The Lane Family
The Barton Farm

for Ba-Ba
with love from
Anthony Barton

Midshipman Harriman

You can feel the wind in your face and Napoleon breathing down your neck. Suddenly you're in the Gulf of Saint Lawrence ready to teach Frigate Captain Jean-Pierre Troude a lesson. But what if somebody finds out who you really are? What if you are wounded in action and carried below to the cockpit? You don't believe any book could be this gripping? Just read three pages and listen for the cries of the gulls.

*FOR
JAN*

ANTHONY BARTON

Midshipman Harriman

Bulmer Press

Midshipman Harriman

Bulmer Press Edition
Copyright © 2013 Anthony Barton
Library and Archives Canada Cataloguing in Publication
Barton, Anthony, 1942- Midshipman Harriman / Anthony Barton
ISBN 978-1-4802-6843-2
I. Title
PS8553.A7776M54 2013 C813'.6 C2012-907732-1
Cover design by Anthony Barton. All Rights Reserved.

This book is sold subject to the condition that it shall not, by way of trade or otherwise, be lent, re-sold, hired out, or otherwise circulated without the publisher's prior consent in any form of binding or cover other than that in which it is published and without a similar condition being imposed on the subsequent publisher.

I

ON the particular night when Corrie and her brother Jim were caught by the press gang and rowed out to His Britannic Majesty's frigate *Swift*, stars danced on the backs of the swells like fireflies while a great bronze moon rose in the east.

Corrie's heart sang as she looked at that rising moon, for it seemed to her a good omen, and she was young enough to crave adventure for adventure's sake, and to rejoice in the unexpected turn of events. Records having been mysteriously erased, we cannot vouchsafe for her age, we know only that she was young enough to pass for a boy. Sad to relate, her brother, having been hit on the head while resisting the press, enjoyed neither the stars nor the moon that night, and Corrie was anxious for him to recover from the blow he had taken so that she and he might discuss the remarkable events that had overtaken them, and consider together, sister and brother, their prospects in the navy.

When a great black cloud came out of nowhere, when a sudden squall descended on the ship's launch, when a crash of thunder reverberated around the natural amphitheater of St. John's harbor, and a bright white flash of light lit up the warship, Corrie clapped her hands with joy. It was like a theater when the curtain rises and you see for the first time the scenery and the actors. It was for her the most dramatic and satisfactory beginning to a career in the Royal Navy that she could possibly imagine. She was beside herself. She was ecstatic.

Corrie followed the sailor carrying the limp body of her brother down a companionway into the bowels of the ship, and entered a world of men, reeking of the unwashed. She was thrilled. She loved the smell of unwashed men. She ducked her head. The only way to move around down here on the gun deck was to walk bent at the waist like a Cornish tin miner, and she estimated the deck head clearance to be about five feet. She saw dim shapes swinging in unison with the restless and unceasing rocking of the ship upon the soft billows of the harbor, and heard the snores of sleeping sailors.

Enjoying every moment of her adventure, she threaded her way among rows of hammocks, and past great black cast iron guns. She was astonished to hear a pig grunt and then the heavy breathing of some larger animal, followed by the restless stamping of a third. Pressing on, she smelled cowpats and the warm breath of cows. A rooster startled her with a loud crowing. There was a panicky scrabble of hens and a flying feather tickled her cheek.

'How is he?' she asked anxiously, as the sailor laid floppy Jim down on the deck.

'Coming round, don't you worry. He'll be himself soon enough,' said the sailor, and then the seamen went about his duties and left her alone with her brother.

'Jim, can you hear me?'

'Headache,' Jim replied thickly.

She watched curiously as her brother felt about with his fingertips. He seemed puzzled by the oak deck and the bits of straw he found there.

'Where?' he croaked. His voice sounded like a frog. There was blood on his lips. Poor Jim. She could hardly wait to tell him what had happened. He was going to be so excited.

'In the *Swift*,' she said. 'Our dream has come true. Isn't that wonderful? This is our ship in the apple tree, come to life. Instead of bunging apples we'll be firing real guns.'

Her brother explored the bump on his skull gingerly with his fingertips. 'I must have come a cropper.'

'The seaman hit you. Don't you remember?'

'Can't see.'

'Don't worry. I can fix your eyes. Just wait until you see where they have put us. We're in the manger with the ship's animals!' She took her handkerchief from her pocket, spat on it, and went to work cleaning some of the blood from her brother's face. His eyelids were gummed together, so she freed them.

'You had better tell them to put you ashore,' said Jim, looking up at her with concern now that he had eyes again, and could think straight.

She shook her head. 'Are you joking? I wouldn't miss this for the world. How soon do you think they'll promote us? I want to be an Admiral as soon as possible. I want to lead whole fleets of ships of the line into battle. I want to fly my own flag. I want to find our parents.'

'You're going to stay?' her brother said, alarmed, and tried to sit up.

She pushed him back down again and put a finger

to her lips. 'Ssh!' she hissed at him. She could hear other pressed men nearby and did not want them to hear her brother say anything about her being a girl.

'God's teeth!' said her brother, staring at her wildly. 'Be serious, Corrie. You can't possibly join the navy. You know why. Don't even think about it. Leave now, while you still can. Go and find the First Lieutenant. Tell him the press gang made a mistake. Go on. I'll be all right. I swear. Get moving, Corrie! I'm serious. You might be killed.'

'I'm not going anywhere. We're in this together. If we die we'll die gloriously, and we'll take piles of Frenchmen with us to our graves. You'll see. It's going to be tons of fun, and the fun is starting right now. I wouldn't miss it for the world. And we'll see the world. The Royal Navy has stations everywhere, not just here in St. John's but all over the world. Think, Jim. We'll see Malta. We'll see Valparaíso. We'll capture Chinese junks and Arab dhows. We'll have oodles of prize money. We'll buy Mrs. Demeter a new edition of the Odyssey.'

Somebody close beside them groaned.

'I'm feeling awful poorly,' the fellow said. He, too, had taken a blow to the head. The press gang had been ruthless.

'What's your name?' asked Jim.

'Campbell.'

'Harriman,' said Jim, and shook hands with the man.

'They'll work us to death from Monday to Saturday, and flog us on Sundays,' said Campbell gloomily, speaking with an accent that made Corrie suspect that he had been born in Edinburgh.

At that moment, something extraordinary and unexpected happened that stirred Corrie deeply, though she was not sure why it moved her so. A lady dressed in white floated by in a rustle of petticoats, a lace trimmed hat tied under her chin with a bow of satin. The lady said not a word in passing and vanished without ceremony into the dark shadows of the fore cockpit. She was perhaps an apparition, or a goddess. Corrie was as thrilled by the sight of this lady as she had been by the sight of the bronze moon. This splendidly attired vision in white was a herald of all Corrie hoped for. Everything about her suggested that she belonged in the *Swift*, and was going about her regular business, whatever the regular business of a goddess might be. In the Odyssey, Pallas Athena took on various guises, sometimes young and sometimes old.

There are women living in a King's ship, then? I have long suspected this, and here is the first evidence. I bubble with hope. There may be a place for me, here. My brother may be wrong to urge me to go ashore before we sail.

Corrie had read a great deal about the navy, her father being a serving officer, but nowhere in any of her father's books had there been more than a passing hint that there might be women serving alongside men in warships. Jim had read those books, too, but she did not think her brother had paid much attention to the occasional references to women, any more than he had noticed the passing of the lady dressed in white a moment ago. His poor head was throbbing. He had closed his eyes to shut out the cruk-cruk-cruk of the capstan pawls as men up on deck put their weight upon the bars, and so he had not seen the vision in white pass by.

She wondered what he would have said if he had.

An officer shouted and there was a patter of bare feet as men ran to make sail.

Corrie crouched down beside her brother, her heart pounding.

I feel goose bumps. There are women in the ship.

She had found tucked away between the leaves of the *Manual of Seamanship* several passages copied in her mother's hand from a scandalous and revolutionary essay by a certain Olympe de Gouges, a free-spirited Frenchwoman who had dared to suggest that women were free with equal rights to men, and that all professions ought to be open equally to men and to women. Corrie had trembled with excitement when she had translated those passages to herself, and just thinking about them today made her tremble again.

'Listen,' she said, shaking her brother's arm urgently. 'Listen to what the sailors are singing.'

> *O, Billy Brown's a bright mullato*
> *Way, ho, roll and go!*
> *Oh, she drinks rum and chews tobacco*
> *Spend my money on Billy Brown!*

The voices fell silent as the din of the capstan

ceased. Corrie heard a thump as the anchor was catted. New orders were shouted above their heads. Corrie felt the deck vibrate as men clambered up into the rigging and ran out along the yards.

'Did you hear what they sang, Jim?' whispered Corrie. 'Billy Brown is a *she*.'

Jim gazed at her askance. They were pressed into the Service and heading for the Narrows. His sister had joined the navy!

Get used to it, brother.

'It's a shanty, Corrie. It doesn't mean anything. It's just a song. I bet Billy Brown doesn't even exist. I bet she's just an imaginary girl the men sing about.'

The deck took on a steeper tilt. The sow squealed and a steer bawled. The animals were frightened.

As the vessel made her first big roll, Corrie heard a plate smash in the galley. She remembered the same thing happening at the start of the voyage she had taken in her uncle's schooner *Maggie Rose*. Some piece of crockery, improperly stowed, had escaped the fiddles.

'We're leaving Cape Spear to starboard,' she said excitedly. 'We're on our way to see our parents. We'll run into them in some foreign port and say "Good morning, Lieutenant Harriman. How are you today, Mrs. Harriman?" and their jaws will drop and they'll gasp with astonishment and then they'll wring our hands and ask us how we are doing, and we'll tell them we've joined the navy.'

Jim stared at her.

He thinks I'm crazy.

For years they had heard nothing from their father

or mother. St. John's was a navy station, so there were many families without fathers, and that was only to be expected. Sometimes years went by while men served in the Mediterranean or in the Caribbean. Sometimes fathers were killed in action or drowned accidentally while handling a small boat in some foreign port, and often their families had to wait for a long time to hear the news.

Their mother being away from home for so long was less easy to explain. Both Corrie and Jim had on many occasions wondered why so much of their schooling had been left to Mrs. Demeter. When they had inquired of their governess, they had been told that 'Your mother would be here for you if she could be.' This evasive answer had raised larger questions in Corrie's mind and had driven her to search her father's library for possible answers. That was how she had come to spend that terrifying afternoon translating Olympe de Gouges. She had not told Jim about that, nor about certain other discoveries she had made. Jim was a man and could not be expected to grasp the peculiar trials and tribulations of women.

'Give me a hand?' asked Jim.

Corrie helped her brother to his feet.

'Come up on deck, Campbell,' Jim suggested to the man next to him. 'The quicker you get your sea legs the better you'll feel.'

Campbell shook his head. 'I'm feared of that Sly,' he said.

'Sly?' Jim asked, raising an eyebrow and looking at his sister. 'Who is Sly?'

'Augustus Sly is the master-at-arms,' said Corrie, eager to fill in the gap in her brother's memory. She knew that it was often true that people who were hit on the head had a hard time trying to recall how they had come to grief. 'Sly was the man who grabbed us in the inn. He had a crony with him, a big hulking brute of a seaman called Foster. They made a nasty pair. I hope we don't meet those two again. I can understand why Campbell here doesn't want to run into them twice in one evening.'

'I don't remember meeting them. I remember we were dancing,' said Jim. *'Three times round went our gallant ship...'* He put a hand to his head.

'That was our song. Better go slowly. Here, take my arm.'

Together they made their way up a ladder of oak and met a goat.

'A-a-a,' said the goat.

'A-a-a to you, too,' said Jim, and he stopped to scratch the animal's head.

Moving more quickly now, Corrie helped Jim up another ladder, and then headed aft, her brother in tow, until they came to a sill designed to prevent sloshing seawater from finding its way below decks.

Beyond the sill lay the open deck. Wind moaned in the rigging. Spindrift was thrown up into the air by the ship's cutwater.

We're at sea. I'm so exhilarated!

'Can you manage?'

Jim nodded. 'I think I can.'

They stepped out into the wind and weather.

II

CORRIE and Jim were hit by a gust that flung them bodily across the deck. They hit something solid, and hung on tightly.

Yow! That hurt.

A single swaying lantern sent darts of light shooting into their eyes.

'Blowing hard,' shouted Jim in her ear.

A wave soused the deck and wet their dancing shoes.

Corrie was filled with energy by the wind and spray.

We're really here. It feels marvelous. I suppose we tempted fate by dancing that hornpipe at the Crown and Anchor. Mrs. Demeter went to so much trouble to make our costumes. Whatever will our governess do when she finds we are gone?

Their dance costumes made them *look* like sailors but the material was too thin to keep them warm.

Corrie shivered again. She and her brother needed warmer, tougher garments; they needed the kinds of jackets and breeches worn by real sailors. But where in the ship were they to find the proper gear to wear? She had no idea.

Another wave burst over the bulwarks and again they clung to the standing rigging. The ropes under her fingers felt as stiff and unyielding as iron bars.

A figure dressed in a pea jacket loomed out of the dark. A flash of sheet lightning lit up the clouds and showed her the scowling visage of the master-at-arms, that horrible and despicable warrant officer who had been so beastly to Jim in the pub. The gloating look in the ship's policeman's piggy eyes told her all she needed to know. This pitiful excuse for a policeman was planning some further beastliness.

Just wait until I'm an Admiral. I'll have this son-of-a-gun flogged around the fleet. Master-at-arms Sly will wish he'd never been born. When the crows are finished with this buffoon, I'll have his guts for garters.

'It's Sly,' she whispered in her brother's ear.

'Well, well!' said the master-at-arms. 'If it ain't the two shavers I collared at the pub. What do you think you're doing up here on deck, eh? That's what I wants to know. Who gave you permission, eh?'

'I needed some fresh air,' said Jim.

'I brought him here, Sly,' said Corrie. 'The responsibility is mine.'

'You address me as Mister Sly, you cheeky little bugger,' said the master-at-arms. 'Foster and me, we're going to teach you two lads to mind your manners, aren't we, Foster? We're going to teach you real good. Being hit on the head wasn't good enough for you, so now we've got something else in mind to put you in your place, something that's going to be a real treat, something that'll make you squeak like the little rats you are.' Sly ran his tongue over his lips. 'What do you say to that, boys?'

'Don't answer him,' said Corrie in her brother's ear. 'He's just a bully.'

Jim balled his fists. He wanted to hit Sly for being rude to his sister but knew that hitting officers was not allowed in the navy, so he kept the peace, and waited, fuming, to see what Sly had in mind for them.

Corrie, too, had read of the importance of obeying orders in the navy. She had studied in detail the stern code of discipline and punishment that was part of everyday life in a warship. She had read the Articles of War. If she were brought before the captain and condemned to be punished, she knew she would be stripped to the waist for a flogging, and then the whole crew of the *Swift* would discover she was a girl and might suspect her of harboring revolutionary ideas.

'Mr. Sly,' she said to the master-at-arms, doing her best to sound respectful. 'We intended no harm. Please allow us to go back to the stable.'

'Why would I want to do that,' said Sly, and he beckoned over his shoulder. 'Come along, Foster. We'll show this pair of miscreants the bilge hole, that's what we'll do. They're going to love the bilge hole.'

The huge sailor Foster stepped out of the shadows, a foolish grin on his face. Foster did not have his billy club with him this time, so far as Corrie could make out, but held instead a lantern shuttered against the wind.

A smile spread slowly across Foster's imbecilic face at the mention of the bilge hole, and Corrie deduced that something particularly unpleasant was awaiting them. She became furious. Her brother needed time to recover his wits. They had no right to subject him to further trials.

If Sly and this fool sailor Foster hurt Jim again, I won't just flog them around the fleet, I'll maroon them on a desert island swarming with crocodiles.

Corrie narrowed her eyes. She supposed that adventurous voyages did not consist entirely of wine-dark seas, summering dawns, and simpering mermaids, but she would explode before she allowed all of their dreams to end in ignominy on this their very first night in the *Swift*, before she and her brother had been granted official status on board. They were not yet members of the crew, for crying out loud.

What was a bilge hole, anyway? Was it some *boy* thing? If they tried to run from Sly and Foster right now, there would be a scuffle, and the two bullies would be sure to discover she was a girl. She did not want *that* to happen.

'He's the master-at-arms,' she said to Jim, striving to keep the anger out of her voice. 'We would be wise to do as he says.'

To this Jim made no reply, beyond raising an eyebrow.

So Sly and Foster hurried Corrie and Jim Harriman below.

Corrie was sure there had been nothing about a bilge hole in her father's library. A ship had bilges. That much Corrie knew, although she could not quite remember what the bilges were or what they were for.

She and Jim were hurried down into a part of the ship she had not seen earlier. She stumbled over a heavy cable that restrained a gun carriage after discharge. She had read in the *Manual of Gunnery and Ballistics* about weapons so powerful that they could kill a dozen men in a single dazzling explosion. Was this where such fiendish devices were stored, deep in the orlop?

Down a set of steps they went, and then down another.

I am Persephone being taken down into Hades. I have entered the Stygian gloom. Mrs. Demeter told us that Persephone sang out for help and was heard by Hekate. I wonder who would hear me if I cried for help now? Not that I am going to do any such thing, for I wouldn't want to give Sly and his accomplice their jollies. I'll just have to make sure those crocodiles on that island are really hungry.

Corrie made a silent vow to herself not to cry out, no matter what horrors awaited her. Jim had told her that boys were expected to face their trials silently, and she was determined to act the part of a boy as convincingly as possible.

Shadows swelled and shrank around her. Timbers groaned. She smelled butter and cheese. A sudden lurch of the ship sent her staggering into a heap of flour sacks.

Here is our ship's store of food. It must take a lot of food to feed so many sailors. I'm glad I'm neither the cook nor the purser.

It would be the job of the ship's purser to know what every sack and every cask contained, and where to find each and every one of them.

She heard a gurgle of hidden waters moving this way and that, and the groans and creaks of the vessel's sides grew louder and more echoey.

'Here we are,' said Sly, sliding aside the shutter of

Foster's lantern to let the light shine down on a trap raised a little above the deck.

O goddess of divine retribution and indignity, spare me. I have a bad feeling about this bilge hole.

'Open her up,' said Sly, grabbing Corrie's arm and Jim's neck while Foster went down on his knees and flung open the trapdoor.

Oh, no. Not this. Please not this. I've never told Jim about my secret fear of water.

Looking down, she had no trouble at all in identifying the bilges and the bilge hole, now that Sly and Foster had been kind enough to show them both to her. It was evident that the hull of the *Swift* was shaped to offer as little resistance to the water as possible, and that her lowermost deck was built flat so as to allow sailors to stow cargo there. Between the flat deck and the curved planks of her hull lay a space that was the last repository of all of the wastewater that drained down from the decks above. The bilges were the lowest internal portions of the hull, and the hole was this trap door that gave access to them.

Corrie gazed down into the hole and felt weak at the knees. She was looking down into the stuff of her own personal nightmares. Sloshing water seethed with swimming rats. The hole smelled of rancid cheese.

So this is what they do to boys. Welcome to the Navy! See if you can stomach this. Ho, ho, ho.

'Down you go,' said Sly.

She turned on Sly. 'I can't stop you from being what you are, Sly, and I can't stop you and Foster from having your little joke. Now enough is enough. Tell

Foster to close up that trap. I'm warning you.'

'Nobody warns me about nothing, you cheeky little imp,' said Sly, and he gave Corrie a powerful shove backwards.

Corrie staggered back, caught her foot on the coaming and fell into the trap. She found herself in a place of unspeakable terror, a place with no up or down, a place that only those of us who have had the most awful things happen to us when we were very young can possibly imagine. The place stirred awful memories for Corrie. She became transfixed with loathing.

I have been to this place before, somewhere near the dawn of my life, and I have revisited it often since. It is a dreadful place, a chamber of horrors, and a place that makes me sick. I curse you, Sly. Those crocodiles aren't good enough for you. I'll have to dream up something far, far worse.

She was gripped by an irrational and profound fear of something she could not see that sought to stifle her. It was an irony of life in the navy that most sailors did not know how to swim, and did not trouble to learn the art. Most believed that if by accident they happened to fall into the water, then their shipmates who did know how to swim would leap into the water to rescue them.

I can't breathe!

In truth, Corrie's fear was as deep as it was well founded. Because of a misadventure in her youth, even the simple act of drinking upset her. Washing her face sapped her courage. She had never told Jim this. She had kept quiet about her weakness with regard to water, not daring to parade that weakness lest others should take advantage of it to persecute her. In this Corrie was no different from you or I, for, whether we recognize them or not, we all have our demons.

Wait until I find out what your weakness is, Sly. Wait until I discover your Achilles' heel. I'll pay you back.

It irked her that Sly took perverse delight in frightening people, while at the same time relishing his position of authority. The man was an insatiable bully.

The foul water closed over her head. She hardly noticed the sharp claws and teeth of the rats as they bit into her arms and legs.

Paralyzed by her very private fear, she froze, and felt a wave of despair roll over her. It was all done with: her dream of entering the navy, her foolish resolve to pretend to be a boy among men, her determination to solve the mystery of why her parents had not been there for her when she was growing up. Her whole life was to end here and now in this filthy bilge hole of the *Swift*, on her very first night.

I'm going to die.

The grim breath-stealing invisible nothing that had once, in her remote past, tried to kill her, had on this night and in this place returned to try again. Her fear was as real and as debilitating as the uncontrollable vertigo some unfortunates feel when they step near to the edge of a cliff. It was not unlike the dire horror others experience when encountering by chance some venomous snake. She experienced trepidation so acute that it rendered her limbs quite useless, and it was as if, faced by death, volition itself had been halted to allow the world to fold up and disappear. Corrie experienced utter despair. She felt she was beyond all help. She was trapped inside herself.

The vision that came to her was clear and sharp. She saw herself standing on the quarterdeck of a ship, dressed in some kind of uniform, while her brother Jim, also in uniform, stood at the wheel, his legs braced and the spokes in his hands. A mountain of water towered before them both. To port, a sheer cliff of some five hundred feet or more loomed, while to starboard she saw a rocky island the size of a cathedral. She heard herself give an order. She saw Jim spin the wheel. She felt the ship's bow begin to rise to meet that liquid mountain. Up, up, up the ship climbed into the sky, seawater pouring from her decks, until she came to the very crest of that vast comber, and Corrie, suspended halfway between heaven and earth, saw the Grey-eyed One smile at her.

As this terrifying vision faded, Corrie's wrath boiled over. What was being done to her in this moment, in this fetid bilge hole in the booming belly of the *Swift*, was wrong not only for her but wrong for all who were new to the Service. If this was the way the navy was, then by God the navy would have to change, and, come hell or high water, it was she, Corrie, who would have to do the changing.

Corrie felt the thump of Jim's body as he joined her in the filthy water, and she lost some precious air from her mouth.

The laughter of the dimwit Foster sounded oddly

deep under the water. Huh-huh-huh.

Foster slammed the trapdoor shut, and she and her brother were left struggling for their lives in utter darkness.

Both of us. I don't believe this. Sly deserves to be shot.

Corrie was majestically wroth. There was far more at stake now than her own pathetic fear of water, and far more at stake than her own life. Now she had her brother Jim to think of, and her ire knew no bounds.

She felt hands tug at her sailor costume.

She surfaced for a moment. She gulped fetid air.

'Jim?' she said, urgently.

'Right here,' her brother replied thickly. That head wound was still giving him trouble.

'Let us out!' she shouted, and pounded on the underside of the trap, but all she heard, by way of a reply, was the scrape of something heavy being dragged on top of the trapdoor to hold it in place.

Her brother joined her in beating on the solid planks of the trap. 'Open this door or you'll be sorry!' he hollered.

Sly must have said something, for Foster laughed once again and then Corrie and Jim heard the footsteps of their tormentors recede, and they were left alone in the unspeakable mire of the ship's bottom water, with no way to open the trapdoor and to free themselves.

How do we get out?

Corrie felt the ship yaw, and heard a roar as tons of filthy water in the *Swift*'s bilges shifted under the pressure of wind and wave, and came pouring back into the confined space where she and Jim crouched.

'Hold your breath!' she cried. 'Hold your nose!'

The ghastly presence pressed in all around her once again. The loathsome liquid felt cold, malignant, and all-powerful. She was knocked off her feet. She clung to her brother, terrified that the water would drag them both away to some spot deep in the ship's bilges. She did her best to help her brother keep his footing.

The ship pitched, and the bilge water drained aft. The bow of the *Swift* rose and Corrie found she could breathe again, but only for a moment. She planted her feet firmly back on the strakes, and grabbed at the frame of the trap with both hands.

It was a grim predicament in which they found themselves. Sly and Foster had for no good reason condemned her brother and herself to an ordeal from which they might not emerge alive. Were the ship to go about, or be laid on her side by a sudden squall, their tiny prison might become flooded and remain flooded for longer than they could hold their breath. The danger was real and imminent.

She gripped Jim by his hair as a fresh wave sent the ship rolling sickeningly to starboard. Once again they were plunged into filth. It was growing harder and harder to think clearly.

Anger and fear are close cousins. Even as the water closed in upon Corrie for a fifth time, even as she braced herself and pushed up hard on the underneath of the trapdoor, and the trap did not budge, a part of her wondered:

What is holding the trap so tightly in place? I have

to know.

As the wave passed under the ship and the vessel rolled back to port, and there came another welcome chance to gasp the unpleasant air, she risked all to blurt out: 'What's holding the trap?'

'Hogshead,' was Jim's curt reply.

Corrie recalled from her reading of *The King's Regulations and Admiralty Instructions Regarding the Provisioning of Ships at Sea* that a 'hogshead' was a cask large enough to hold more than sixty gallons of wine. Yes, she imagined that a barrel that big would be enough dead weight to keep any trapdoor closed. 'How do we move the hogshead?'

'Can't,' said Jim. 'It would take two grown men like Sly and Foster to shift it. Ow! Curse these rats!'

Corrie had an inspiration then, and she said: 'If we can't move the cask, I'll bet you the *Swift* can move the cask for us.'

'Corrie, you're amazing,' said Jim, and he meant it.

'I'm wildly angry, that's all,' said Corrie. 'One of these days I'm going to make that Sly wish he'd never been born, but right now you and I have to move that hogshead. That cask must be standing on its own.' She paused to spit out a mouthful of waste. 'If the cask is standing on its own... Damn! Here comes the water again.'

The ship, having pitched and rolled, now yawed, sending the reeking slop water rushing back once more to fill the tiny compartment.

Rotting detritus stung Corrie's eyes. Rats scratched her forehead.

I'll pay you back for this, Sly. One day you'll be sorry. I wish I could see Jim. I can't see a cursed thing.

She waited, holding her breath, until the water drained away, and then took a quick deep breath and braced her feet against the ship's bottom. 'We have to work together to give the cask a nudge,' she said.

'Right,' said Jim.

The ship shouldered aside another wave, the rats squeaked, and Corrie and Jim pressed their hands to the trapdoor above their heads. They waited, intent upon their fingertips.

'Feel that?' Corrie asked. 'When the ship rolls, the hogshead shifts. If we push upwards on this end of the trap, maybe we can help the cask shift even further. Are you ready? When I give the word.'

'Ready,' said Jim, and he tensed himself.

III

THROUGH the soles of her feet, Corrie sensed the ship's stern slide down into a trough between two waves. The fabric of the ship shuddered as she met the next swell of seawater, and then the bow rose, straining, towards the sky.

Corrie closed her eyes. So powerful was her imagination, and so great her affinity with the vessel, it was as if she could feel the wind pressing harder and harder upon the masts, the sails and the standing rigging. For a moment Corrie felt as if she *was* the ship. She felt the deck cant. The vessel leaned further and further to starboard. The hogshead on top of the trapdoor began to move. 'Now!' she cried. 'Push, Jim! Push like the devil!'

Corrie and her brother put their backs to the underneath of the trapdoor and straightened their legs. Legs are more powerful than arms. They felt the trapdoor give.

'Harder!' cried Corrie.

The filthy water came flooding back to choke them, but they paid no heed to it and went on straining away. The trapdoor began to shake. They heard a grinding, scraping noise. The cask was moving!

'Again!' cried Corrie. 'Heave!'

Once more they pushed with all their might.

The sound of the ship's bell came to Corrie faintly, transmitted through the fabric of the ship. Ting-ting. Ting-ting. Four Bells in the Middle Watch.

We're winning. I'm going to get us out of this.

Again the pair took the dreadful strain, and again they timed their effort to coincide with the tilting of the vessel, and now the grinding and scraping grew much louder and went on a great deal longer.

They pushed and strained again and went on pushing and straining until at last the cask slid free, the trap flew back with a mighty crack, and Corrie and Jim scrambled up out of the bilge hole and into the murkiness of the hold, and lay side by side on the deck sucking in great mouthfuls of air. They were safe. They were out. They had escaped from Sly's abominable trap.

When they had fully recovered, Corrie had the common sense to say: 'We should put the trapdoor back in place. It's dark down here, and we don't want anyone to have an accident.' She felt about for the trap cover, and found the edge of it. 'Help me.'

'The hole's over here,' said Jim's voice.

She slid the cover towards him in the dimness, and together they covered the bilge hole.

'What about the hogshead?' Jim asked, and Corrie heard her brother pat the curved side of the huge barrel. 'We can't leave it unsecured. We ought to try to jam it into some narrow place.'

'Good idea,' said Corrie. All movable objects had to be stowed when at sea.

The giant cask was a brute to move standing on its end, but by tilting it a little, they found they could 'walk' it on its rim. The cask hit the deckhead and would go no further.

'That will have to do,' said Corrie. Her unspoken

terror of the water was ebbing away, but her fury at Sly was still with her.

A fighting service needed fighters, and if Sly tried any more of his tricks, she would show him she was a fighter. She was not sure how, but she would fight him. In her opinion, Sly was a pain in the neck and a disgrace to his ship. The man should never have been appointed master-at-arms in the first place.

'We need a bath and a change of clothes,' she said. 'We should find the ship's laundry.'

'The laundry is usually near the heads,' said Jim.

'Let's go and look for it,' said Corrie, and they made their way through the maze of steps and storerooms until they came to the bowsprit and there, as Jim had predicted, was an airy washing space, open to both the night sky and the sea. The ship's laundry contained a big wooden tub, held in place by stanchions to prevent it from sliding across the deck. The tub was half-full of soapy water that sloshed back and forth with the unceasing motion of the ship, but it was not the laundry tub that impressed Corrie so much as the two huge women on their knees on either side of the tub, wringing out a pair of trousers by the light of a flickering beef tallow candle.

Both women looked up as Jim and Corrie came in.

'New faces,' said one.

'You two look like you was up all night,' said the other.

'We've been in the bilges,' said Jim, shortly. He was tired and his head still hurt.

Corrie took a quick glance at her brother and

judged that the presence of these strapping women, hard at work here in the middle of the night, had come as a bit of a shock to him, too.

Then she recalled how Admiral St. Vincent had put his foot in his mouth by complaining about the amount of fresh water used by the ship's women for washing. He had explained to an astonished public that fresh water was worth its weight in gold, a precious commodity better poured down the throats of thirsty sailors than wasted by laundresses. Here were two of those laundresses of whom the Admiral had spoken so disparagingly, pausing in their work to look at a pair of bedraggled and smelly sailors who had just entered their laundry.

Corrie lifted her chin and returned their gaze as best she could, wondering if these giant women would be able to tell she was a girl by the look of her face. She feared her voice might give her away. Suppressing her misgivings, she put on a confident, boy-like air, as if she had every right to be there, walked up to them boldly and asked brightly 'May we wash our clothes?'

'Lord save us!' said the first woman. 'What a reek! Did you ever smell the like, Norah?'

'Never in my life, Gladys. One more squeeze and we're done.'

Together Norah and Gladys wrung the last drops of water from the twisted trousers. 'What were you two boys doing down in the bilges?' asked Norah.

Corrie and Jim looked at one another. They had learned in the *Maggie Rose* that everything said on a crowded vessel quickly becomes general knowledge, and they were not sure they wanted their visit to the bilge hole to become the subject of gossip that might give Sly and his dimwit bullyboy Foster an excuse to devise further ingenious 'punishments.'

Neither Corrie nor Jim answered Norah's question but instead stared back at the laundresses with what they hoped were stony, impassive faces.

Norah regarded the pair shrewdly. 'That bastard Augustus Sly,' she said quietly. 'Up to his old tricks, I'll be bound.'

That was interesting. Norah did not need to be told.

Gladys smiled at them. 'Never you mind, lads. We'll wash your clothes for you, but you'll need something dry and warm to wear while you're waiting. Help yourselves from the purser's slops,' she said, and waved a fat arm at a canvas bin stuffed with new clothes.

Corrie's face lit up. Her anger gave way to exhilaration and hope. This was more like it. This was what she had been waiting for. This was the Royal Navy of her dreams. Here was the beginning of her new life. Here was the opportunity to change out of the silly sailor costume in which she had danced and sung at the inn and to don instead the working clothes of a real sailor, clothes that would make it easier for her to hide the fact that she was a woman. She stretched her arms wide, expanded her chest, and breathed in the bracing night air. She rejoiced in the heaving of the sea and the wind singing in the rigging.

I'm the luckiest girl in the world.

By the time the sun rose in the morning she would

look the part she intended to play, if only she could find some way to change here in this airy laundry without revealing her gender to Norah and Gladys.

First things first, she decided, and went to the bin. She rummaged about among the slops, looking for clothes that would best disguise her gender. She picked out a warm sailor's jacket with a score of buttons down the front, a pair of breeches that ended below the knee, and a japanned hat that was just her size. Unlike the ship's officers, the ordinary and able seamen were not expected to wear any special uniform, but instead came to rely on various articles of clothing commonly sold by pursers and known in the navy as 'slops,' but because these slops came from the same tailors' shops on the same waterfronts, there were similarities in the way the seamen dressed.

Corrie chose items typical of those worn on the lower deck. She felt that the jacket might make her look like a boy by covering up the more rounded parts of her body. Her long hair would go unremarked, for many sailors wore their hair long. She hoped the hat would serve both to shade her face and to make her smooth chin and rounded cheeks less obvious.

With a bit of luck those who saw her would see what they expected to see: a young man, and not what she was in truth: a young woman. It was a little annoying that she could not dress as she pleased, but Corrie was a pragmatist at heart. If these slops would help her serve in the navy, then she would wear them. But how to change into these new clothes without catching the eye of Norah and Gladys? That was the problem. Then it dawned on her that she was supposed to be a *boy* and so she would be *expected* to want to wash and change out of sight of Norah and Gladys! Sometimes the answer to a problem is simpler than you think.

If I do whatever my brother does, then they'll think I'm a boy, too. Wahoo, wahoo!

Jim picked out the clothes he wanted to wear, made a bundle of the new clothes he had chosen in his arms, and then looked about for somewhere private to wash and change. He saw a blanket pegged to a clothesline and stepped behind that hanging screen for privacy. Corrie joined him there, reminding herself that since she was supposed to be a boy, Norah and Gladys would not be shocked to see her join her brother in his ablutions behind the blanket.

The sea was loud and wonderful here on this side of the blanket. She pulled off her stinky clothes and stood in the buff balanced upon two stout timbers that projected from the ship's side, and got a charge out of standing naked in the sharp night air, balanced precariously upon this lofty perch where the crew came to answer the call of nature. After her humiliation in the bilge hole, we may forgive Corrie if she felt a certain savage satisfaction as she relieved herself at the expense of her greatest enemy, the unrelenting ocean. Even when gazing straight down at the waves, she could see little of the foe she feared so deeply, just a few white flecks of foam hurrying by.

Now I'll wash myself sailor-fashion.

She returned to more solid footing and discovered

a metal laundry pail hanging from a davit. She made sure that there was a line made fast to the handle, and then upended the bucket and let it drop into the sea with its bottom uppermost, a trick her uncle had shown her on the *Maggie Rose*. As soon as she heard the bucket hit the sea, she twitched the line, waited a moment or two to let the bucket fill, and then hauled it back up hand over hand. The pail felt heavy with the weight of the water. She put the bucket down with a thump on the deck, and felt a stab of fear.

At any moment Norah or Gladys may glance over the top of the blanket and discover that I'm not a boy.

She dipped a bar of ash-and-fat laundry soap into the bucket of water and scrubbed her body furiously from head to toe. The rat bites and scratches on her legs smarted, but it felt wonderful to be free at last of the horrid stench of that bilge hole.

She tossed the bar of soap to Jim, emptied the bucket of seawater over her head and fetched up a fresh bucket of seawater for her brother. She watched as he emptied the bucket over himself. The blood from the welt on his head had matted his hair, but otherwise he looked fit and ready for more adventures.

I have a strong brother. He is recovering fast from what that brute Foster did to him.

'That feels better,' she said, shaking her head and looking around for towels. There were none. Their bodies would have to dry by themselves.

Corrie and Jim pulled on their new clothes as fast as they could. Corrie's fingers fumbled several times with the unfamiliar buttons. She did not see why there had to be so many buttons on a sailor's jacket. When they had finished dressing, they turned to look at one another and burst out laughing.

Corrie had chosen breeches with vertical blue and white stripes, and a dark blue jacket with a high collar that turned up. She looked like a slender and agile boy.

Jim had chosen an olive jacket with bright brass buttons. He looked like a Paris revolutionary.

'What would Mrs. Demeter say?' said Corrie.

'She'd never let us go to the pub again,' said Jim.

They both giggled.

Is my brother jealous? I think so. A little bit.

Corrie knew that Jim had ever really expected that his sister would join the navy. Now that they were both sailors, he was probably both envious of her and fearful for her. He knew as well as she did that the appalling master-at-arms would soon learn of their escape from the bilge hole, and that he was bound to come looking for them, probably with murder on his mind. People like Sly never leave well alone. She could hardly blame Jim for wishing he did not have a sister to look after.

It hasn't dawned on Jim that I may just end up looking after him, instead of the other way around. If that turns out to be the case, then I fear he is going to be hopping mad.

Grinning at the thought, she bundled together their discarded hornpipe dancing costumes, his and hers, and carried them at arm's length to the laundry tub. 'Thanks so much,' she said, and she smiled at Norah.

'No problem,' said Norah.

'They'll be ready by morning,' said Gladys.

'May we have a drink of water?' asked Jim. 'I'm awfully thirsty.'

'Help yourself,' said Gladys, and she waved at the barrel of fresh water that was used for washing shirts. 'You didn't tell us your names.'

'I'm Jim Harriman and this – ' he paused, confused. He had never had trouble introducing his sister before, but now that she was his brother he found himself tongue-tied.

'I'm Corrie,' said his sister, coming to his rescue. She was thankful that her name was one given to both men and women, so that she did not have to answer to a new name in order to keep up her masquerade.

A wooden dipper hung by a cord beside the water barrel. She dipped the scoop into the fresh water, suddenly conscious that she, too, was awfully thirsty. Perhaps it was the salt in the air. Her last drink had been in the Crown and Anchor. The pub seemed far, far away now, part of another world where the floor stood still.

The dipper came up thick and green with living things. She swallowed gulp after gulp, too tired to be frightened. Her struggle down in that hell of a bilge hole had left her weary, and her brother looked about ready to pass out. That sore head of his had to be pounding away inside his skull, demanding that he rest.

She put the dipper back in its rack and sank to her knees. Was there anywhere she and Jim could sleep? Had anybody allotted them hammocks? Her brain did not seem to be working.

The deck came up to meet her.

She felt the caulking of the deck under her cheek. It smelled of tar and oakum.

'Lie down before the bully-bagger comes to get you,' said the voice of her governess.

Corrie tried to raise her head but her head would not move.

If I can't move my head, then I must be asleep. Something is crawling over the rail. My God, it's a huge crab! I can see the beast's pincers opening a shutting. This must be the biggest crab in the whole world. The crab is crawling towards me sideways. It is waving its front legs. I can see the crab's eyes bouncing about on the end of long stalks. The crab's mouth is opening and closing. I can hear the crab singing a song.

As Corrie lay there with her head cradled on her arms, listening to the crab singing its song, the *Swift* bore away from the coast of the island of Newfoundland, and the sky lightened a little in the east, giving a hint of the coming dawn. The rain petered out and the clouds parted to reveal the planet Venus bright and unwavering in an indigo heaven.

Norah and Gladys finished washing the clothes, and then stood side by side for a moment to look down upon the two young people sleeping on the deck.

'Bless them,' said Gladys. 'That Sly should be ashamed.'

'I'll have a word with Anne in the morning,' said Norah.

The two women left.

The night wore on.

IV

HOURS later, Corrie woke with a start.

'Them's the two,' she heard a voice say. 'They stole them clothes they're wearing. Arrest them!'

Corrie scrambled to her feet.

'Jim!' she said, grabbing her brother's arm. 'Wake up! It's him.'

Her brother, startled, jumped up and stood beside her. He was white-faced and looked bemused by sleep. 'Mr. Sly,' he said, facing the man who had pushed his sister into the bilge hole, and digging his fingernails into the palms of his hands.

Corrie frowned. Sly had not brought the stupid Foster with him this time, but had brought along instead a burly Royal Marine sergeant who made an impressive figure, wide-shouldered and resplendent in a scarlet jacket, with checked shirt, brown trousers, gaiters and brightly polished shoes.

'We're not thieves,' Corrie said as loudly and clearly as she could, for she was determined to counter this serious accusation that Sly was making. Sly was making a charge so grave that it had to be denied at once and denied most firmly. In the Old Bailey, the penalty for stealing a sheep or a handkerchief was death, and in the navy, where sailors lived at close quarters and had few possessions, there was a natural aversion to thievery. The Royal Marines, who were the navy's soldiers, tended to feel that the best way to deal with a thief was first to expose him, and then to haul him before the authorities so that he might be condemned on the spot and hanged as soon as was possible, preferably from a yardarm in sight of all, to discourage other thieves.

Corrie looked into the eyes of the marine. She did not think she had seen this man the night before. He had not been part of the press gang, nor had there been any sign of him on deck when she had joined the ship. She could see suspicion in the marine's eyes, and there was something about the smallness of his forehead that hinted at a lack of imagination. Her dream could end like this. Her career could be over, her life forfeit. Clearly that was what Sly intended. While she had been sleeping, Sly must have gone down to the bilge hole, found it empty, and then searched the ship from stem to stern. When he had found them asleep in the laundry, he had summoned this marine sergeant to arrest them.

'Wot are your names?' said the marine.

'Harriman, sergeant. I'm Corrie Harriman and this is my brother Jim Harriman.'

Did her voice sound like a girl? Would they find out who she really was now, or hang her first and then find out?

There was a different feeling about the movement of the deck under her feet, and a change in the quality of the light creeping into the laundry. The blankets, hanging from the lines and swaying this way and that with the canting of the ship, looked bluer and less yellowy than she remembered. The tallow had burned right out. She must have slept for hours. Dawn was coming soon, and she was afraid that it would be the last dawn she would ever see. She swallowed. In all the books she had read, people were hanged at dawn. She had no idea why.

'Wot's your rating?' said Sergeant Deering.

Corrie knew what the sergeant meant by this question. Sailors in the navy are ranked as to competence. An 'Ordinary Seaman' is entrusted with undemanding duties such sanding and scrubbing the deck, while an 'Able Bodied Seaman' may be asked to perform more specialized tasks such as the maintenance of the blocks and sheaves. The marine wished to know what kind of people he was dealing with.

'We haven't been rated yet,' said Corrie. 'We are newly pressed men and haven't signed the muster book.'

'These your clothes?' asked the sergeant, taking hold of the cuff of Corrie's jacket between his thumb and finger and giving the garment a shake.

'They're from slops,' she replied, holding her head high so as not to appear guilty.

A look of self-satisfaction stole across Sergeant Deering's face. 'From slops, you say? How much did the purser charge you for them?' The sergeant narrowed his eyes and regarded Corrie craftily.

'I don't know what you mean,' said Corrie, who was at war with a sinking feeling in her stomach. 'We haven't met the purser.'

'You stole these here clothes behind the purser's back, then,' the sergeant said, looking thoroughly pleased with himself. 'Serious matter, stealing. Hang you for that, I wouldn't be surprised.'

'But we didn't know we weren't supposed to take

the clothes,' said Jim, staring aghast at the marine.

Corrie watched her brother run his hand though his hair and saw his fingers catch in the clotted blood. 'The women in the laundry said we could help ourselves,' she said, wondering if she was allowed to mention the fact that there *were* women doing the laundry.

'Save your excuses for the master,' said the sergeant. 'Thank you, Mr. Sly. I'll take these two lads from here. Follow me!'

Corrie and Jim followed the marine sergeant out of the laundry and headed aft from the forecastle and along the upper deck, leaving behind them the soap-and-water smells of the laundry. Already the sailors had begun their day's work in the pre-dawn light. Looking about her with interest, Corrie saw seamen upending buckets of seawater on the deck while others dragged a hairy coir mat weighed down with ballast across the deck to scour the white pine planking clean. The seamen sang as they worked:

> *They call me hanging Johnnie*
> *They say I hangs for money*
> *They call me Hanging Johnnie*
> *So hang, boys, hang!*

Corrie and Jim followed the marine sergeant along the deck past the great column of the mainmast, where Corrie saw the falls of the countless halyards, all neatly coiled with their ends tidily frapped. Would she ever have the chance to learn the names of those halyards, and to distinguish one from another? The smaller lines were for hoisting signals or pennants to the masthead. One of the smaller lines might be for stringing up offenders accused of stealing. She shivered.

Corrie wondered what the noose would feel like when they put it around her neck and drew it tight. Whose face would be the last she saw? Would it be that of her brother? Or would it be that of the gloating Augustus Sly? And what happened after you died? Did you go somewhere? Did you wake up like Odysseus in some drowsy land of lotus-eaters? What good was her disguise now? Man or woman, she would die just the same.

They followed the sergeant into the quarters of the marine detachment where his fellows were pipe-claying their belts and applying spirits of hartshorn to remove stains from their uniforms. It looked as though the ship's soldiers were getting ready for an inspection.

The sergeant spoke a few words to his men, somebody cracked a joke Corrie did not understand, and then the sergeant led Corrie and Jim up the companionway outside the captain's cabin. They emerged onto the quarterdeck, and Corrie, despite the threat hanging over her, felt a surge of excitement. She was striding across the deck from which the *Swift* was commanded! Here was the wheel. Here was the helmsman with his hands on the spokes and a quid of tobacco in his mouth that made his cheek bulge. Here was the officer of the watch, the same lieutenant who had led the shore party to raid the Crown and Anchor. The lieutenant stood there, hands behind his back, while a younger officer stood at a respectful distance behind him. Corrie knew the younger man was a midshipman by the white patch on the collar of his uniform coat. He was handsome, and he had a spyglass tucked under his arm.

To whom was the marine sergeant taking them? Were they being taken to meet the officer of the watch? Were they being taken to meet the midshipman? No, they were not. They were marched past both of these officers to a man she had not seen before, and were halted before this stranger. For a moment Corrie thought this might be the commanding officer of the *Swift*, but she was mistaken. Two good-for-nothing boys accused of stealing from the slops hardly merited such lofty attention.

'Here's the master who'll hear your case,' said Sergeant Deering. 'Stand up straight now,' he said sharply to Corrie and Jim, and then he came to attention himself, and saluted the ship's master and said: 'Miscreants, Mr. Weevil. Two young boys caught stealing clothes in the laundry.'

Corrie broke out in a sweat.

Nothing can save us now. I'm going to be hanged, and Jim is going to die with me. This wrinkly old Mr. Weevil is the sailing master, the warrant officer charged with the navigation of the ship. He is the second most important officer aboard, and the man we have to answer to. He is the judge who will decide if we live or die, and one look at Mr. Weevil's face is enough to tell me we are not going to be spared. I'm so sorry, Jim. I got us into this. I said the wrong thing to the sergeant, and now it has come to this.

The master stood close to the binnacle, perhaps to save himself from a fall if the ship should make a sudden, unexpected movement. The old man looked as though he might keel over at any moment.

Always curious, even when in peril of her life, Corrie stared with admiration at the instrument. It was mounted on a sturdy post. She could just make out the compass card under the glass, and by leaning forwards slightly on her toes, she was able to catch a fleeting glimpse of the trembling needle that swung fitfully this way and that with the vagaries of the waves, and yet pointed always in the general direction of the magnetic north pole, guided, so her uncle had assured her, by an unseen force that permeated the ether.

The master was hatless, silver-haired, with a face covered in wrinkles. He wore a black choker at his neck and a gentleman's coat with a buttoned waistcoat in an ochre and gold stripe, but there was an air about him that led Corrie to suspect that he was not really a gentleman, despite the fine silver chain dangling from his fob, doubtless attached to a chronometer. A good watch was useful in the accurate determination of longitude to the nearest degree and minute.

'Stealing clothes from the laundry?' said the master, and frowned sternly at Corrie.

'Permission to speak, sir?' said Corrie, greatly daring.

'Granted,' said Mr. Weevil, and cocked his head to one side as if to hear better.

Corrie's heart sank.

He's deaf. I had better raise my voice.

'Came aboard last night, sir,' she shouted. 'This is my brother. Had to change clothes, sir. Didn't know what to do. Helped ourselves to clothes from the slops, sir.'

'You can't help yourselves to clothes from the slops without seeing the purser first,' said Mr. Weevil pontifically.

'Sorry, sir,' hollered Corrie. 'Didn't know, sir. Waiting to be rated and assigned, sir.'

Corrie saw Mr. Weevil put his tongue in his cheek and root about, probably trying to dislodge some sliver of salt beef that had become stuck between his teeth, if he had any teeth.

'You seem to know something of the navy,' said Mr. Weevil.

'Our father taught us about the Service, sir,' yelled Corrie.

'Ah,' said Mr. Weevil, looking thoughtfully over the heads of the two boys and past the shoulder of the marine sergeant at some wheeling and bawling gulls that were fighting over scraps thrown out by the ship's cook.

Corrie, waiting to be sentenced to death, thought that the decrepit Mr. Weevil was casting his mind back over his long years in the navy, and she hoped he had not lost his memory as well as his hearing.

'Harriman. Harriman. Let me see,' said the master. 'Yes, I do recall serving with a Harriman in the *Queen Charlotte.*'

Corrie was not sure what to say. Perhaps it would be better if she said nothing. Her father *had* served in the *Queen Charlotte*, and might still be serving in that fine ship, for all she knew. She had never heard her father speak of a shipmate named Weevil, but if the old deaf master of the *Swift* wanted to think that her father was one of his past shipmates, then let him. Anything that might save her brother and herself from hanging was just fine with her. She nodded twice, firmly, and said a silent prayer.

'I can't make any exceptions,' said Mr. Weevil. 'I have to do my duty. There can be no special favors.'

Corrie's last hope faded. They were condemned. It was all over. Poor Jim. Her mind raced, trying out a dozen wild schemes to save their lives. They could seize the ship, or seize Mr. Weevil and hold him for ransom, but she knew in her heart of hearts that no act of rebellion would succeed in prolonging their lives by more than an hour or two, and so she decided to die with dignity. 'Yes, Mr. Weevil,' she shouted. 'Please go ahead and do what you have to do.'

'Sergeant Wilkes,' said the master.

'Deering, sir. Sergeant Deering.'

'Sergeant Deering, of course. You did the right thing in bringing these boys to me. Please give my compliments to the purser, and tell him I should like to see him as soon as may be convenient. Tell him to bring his book.'

'Yes, sir. You wants to see the purser at once, with his book,' said the sergeant, and, having repeated the instructions given him, he saluted smartly, spun on his heel and marched off, his polished footwear leaving boot polish marks on the freshly scrubbed deck.

At that moment a spark of intense white light appeared on the horizon. Dawn was breaking. The purser had been sent for, and was to bring his book. Corrie was sure she knew what that implied. The names of her brother and herself would be recorded in the purser's book before the official execution was carried out.

Mr. Weevil fished a silver watch from his waistcoat pocket and regarded the timepiece thoughtfully. He glanced at the sun and then back at his watch.

Corrie knew that the time of sunrise for every day of the year was listed in the *Nautical Almanac*. The exact time of her own death, and that of her brother, would be noted. Until then she would relish being alive and standing here on the quarterdeck. All about her the heavens were blushing. The sky was glowing with healthy radiance. No wonder Homer wrote about fingertips of rose making the world bright! Before Corrie's eyes the waters of the ocean began to jump madly with dazzling sparks of carmine and tangerine. Corrie let her breath out slowly, hardly daring to believe that such a wonder was hers to enjoy in these her last moments on Earth.

Now I know why they hang people at dawn.

She lowered her gaze. How strange that she would never again watch the shadows of the shrouds slide back and forth making these lovely patterns on the deck. She watched a gull land on the ship's rail, and was astonished by its soft, smooth feathers.

I have never really looked at birds. Birds have no

hands. They do everything with their beaks. There is so much I have left to learn about the world, and so little time left to take it all in.

Looking about her, Corrie noticed that for those not sentenced to die, life went on as usual. The officer of the watch said something to the man at the wheel about the smells coming from the galley and the sailor shifted his quid and said 'Spotted Dick.' The midshipman found this hilarious and earned a reprimand from Mr. Weevil.

Over there by the taffrail two women were talking earnestly. One was Norah, the big Scottish girl whom Corrie had met in the laundry, and the other was the lady in white whom Corrie had seen pass by in the night. She was a slender person dressed in a striking gown with palmetto borders, cut in the 'antique' style that was all the rage in London and Paris, with a matching beribboned hat that was broad-brimmed and tied with a satin bow. Was she a passenger? Or the wife of one of the ship's officers?

Corrie was transfixed.

I should have liked very much to have met her, but my time is running out.

The lady in question, having listened to what Norah had to say, turned and gazed thoughtfully straight at Corrie.

Corrie gasped.

I can't believe she's looking right at me.

Corrie stared back.

Are the two women talking about me? I think they are.

Corrie's heartbeat quickened. Whatever were they saying? Had Norah peeped over the top of that blanket in the laundry? Did Norah know that Corrie was a girl? What were the two women talking about? They were too far away for Corrie to hear.

The lady in the hat turned and asked Norah a further question.

By way of an answer Norah pointed up at a wooden platform attached to the lower mainmast, a platform built for observation and for the attachment and adjustment of halyards.

Corrie felt weak at the knees. The women were here to witness the hanging.

They have come up on deck early to see me die.

V

CORRIE saw the lady wearing the hat beckon to a boy of about ten years of age who was skylarking with his friends in the mizzen ratlines.

The child abandoned his game, leapt lightly to the deck and ran over to her.

Watching the calm manner in which the child looked up at the lady in white, and the intensity with which he listened to what she had to say, Corrie thought the boy might be her son.

The lady made the child repeat what she had told him and then made a hurry-up gesture.

The child ran to the main shrouds, clambered up the lines with the quickness and agility of a monkey, leapt up onto the platform and vanished from sight.

Corrie wondered what message the boy was carrying and to whom he was carrying it.

The two women were looking at her again. They seemed to be waiting for something to happen.

I think they are waiting for the hangman to arrive.

Corrie looked up at the platform again. A lithe, dark-skinned sailor descended from the futtock shrouds to the deck with natural agility and grace. The sailor's motions were so practiced and so economical, and the sailor made so little fuss about coming down to the deck, that Corrie was filled with admiration and not a little envious. The sailor made climbing down from the platform look easy.

She watched the sailor cross the deck and approach the master. The sailor waited patiently, hat off, for the master to look up from his chronometer.

'Yes, Brown?' said the master, stuffing his watch back in his fob.

Corrie stiffened. She put a hand to her mouth.

The sailor's name is Brown! Could this be the Billy Brown of whom the sailors sang when we weighed anchor?

Corrie's heart began to beat wildly. Was this sailor Brown a man or a woman? She could not tell. She darted a quick glance at the two women by the taffrail. There was something tense about both of them.

Corrie returned her attention to Brown.

'I want two new boys to train for the maintop, Mister Weevil,' Brown was saying.

'These two old enough?' asked the master, waving his hand at Corrie and Jim.

'They'll do,' said Brown.

'Then they are yours,' said the master.

As soon as these words reached Corrie's ears, she raised her elbows up high and began the hornpipe motion with her hands while jigging away with her legs as she sang: '*Three times round went our gallant ship, and three times round went she…*'

Her brother Jim joined in cheerfully, making the same moves with his hands while he sang: '*And the third time she went round, she sank to the bottom of the sea.*'

They ended their impromptu dance by springing into the air like a pair of spring lambs and butting their heads together. It was a trick that had gone down well at the Crown and Anchor, and it went down well with the watching sailors in the rigging of the *Swift*, who, having watched agape the strange goings on down on the quarterdeck, broke out into spontaneous applause and wolf-whistles.

Even the midshipman became carried away. He tried a few jigs of his own, threw his hat into the air, and gave a cheer.

'We're not going to die!' cried Corrie, bubbling with relief and happiness. 'We're not going to be hanged!'

'I know,' said Jim, smiling into his sister's eyes.

It was an exciting moment for all concerned, but a shocking lapse in discipline.

The officer of the watch was not about to ignore such goings-on.

'Mr. Potts,' roared Lieutenant Keeper, 'kindly remember who you are and where you are. Mr. Weevil. I'd be obliged if you would read these new hands in and teach them to behave themselves. We're a ship of war, not a theatre of fools!'

'You hot-steppers, you stand steady,' said Billy Brown.

'I'll rate them Ordinary Seamen,' said the master. 'Here comes the purser now.'

A gentleman of middle years ran up the companionway steps. He was dressed in a Puritan high felt hat of the style much admired in England, a white neckcloth, a shirt collar with sharp parricides, and ink-stained lace cuffs that protruded from his coat sleeves. He carried a brown leather portmanteau bound with two leather straps tucked tidily under his arm. As he strode across the quarterdeck to join them, his pinch-me spectacles wobbled upon a prodigious nose worthy of a Wellington. In his free hand the purser carried a left-handed sharpened goose quill and a bottle of powdered ink that he had mixed with water.

The purser spoke: '*How fast has brother followed brother, from sunshine to the sunless land.* These, I take it, are the two brothers?' The purser laughed at his own joke, which Corrie did not understand, and made saucer eyes at Corrie and Jim. '*Two owls with necks revolving*, by the look of them. What a pair!'

The master was affronted. 'They are the sons of an old shipmate of mine, Lieutenant Harriman, and they have come to join the navy, Mr. Hartnell,' said the master severely. 'I'd be obliged if you would read them in. They have, as you can see, helped themselves to some of your Slops.'

'For that they shall pay dearly,' said Mr. Hartnell. He gave Corrie a wink and whipped his portmanteau from under his arm, freed the straps of a great leather bound portfolio which he flipped opened upon the binnacle. He licked his quill, unscrewed the cap of his inkbottle, dipped quill in ink and said 'I dare say you lads cannot sign your own names? Shall I sign on your behalf?'

'We can both write,' said Jim. He was not taken with the purser.

'Where do I sign, Mr. Hartnell?' Corrie asked, putting out a hand for the quill.

'Here if you please,' replied the purser. 'Underneath *James Campbell, ORD, his mark.*'

Corrie ran her eye over the muster roll. James Campbell's mark was a shakily penned 'X' very like many of the other marks scrawled on the page by recently pressed men to signify their enrolment in the ship's company and in what was arguably the most efficient navy in the world, even if few of its sailors could read or write.

She added her own name to the list, Corrie Harriman, and after her name she added the letters ORD to signify 'Ordinary Seaman.'

She felt a tingle of excitement.

I've joined the navy. Now they'll have to pay me.

She was glad her Christian name was not one ascribed to a gender. Had she been baptized with a name like 'Mary' or 'Elizabeth,' she would have had to call herself 'John' or 'Sam.'

Did Mum and Dad choose my name to be ambiguous?

It was a startling thought.

She handed over the quill to Jim and watched him write his name JAMES HARRIMAN, in the muster roll. His writing was rounder than hers, but quite as felicitous. He, too, added the letters ORD for 'Ordinary Seaman' after his name, just as she had done, and then returned the goose quill and inkbottle to Mr. Hartnell.

'Scholars of the lower deck!' cried the purser, admiring their handwriting as he dusted their entries with finely powdered pounce that he pinched from a small alabaster box fished from his waistcoat pocket. 'You have fair hands, both of you. I shall employ you in my accounts department making copies of my ledgers, if Mr. Weevil approves.' He closed the alabaster box with a snap and returned it to his pocket.

'Too late, Mr. Hartnell,' said the master. 'Twopence for a jacket and threepence for a hat! You would do better to keep your shenanigans to yourself. Take your muster book and be gone.' The master snatched the portmanteau from the binnacle and thrust it back into the arms of the purser.

'*At every word a reputation dies*,' said the purser ruefully, 'but I shall have these two for my office. You may count on it. I shall not be gainsaid.'

'You are too late, as I told you, Hartnell,' the master retorted. 'These boys are spoken for. Billy Brown here needs them in the maintop.' The master tilted his head to indicate the dark-skinned sailor standing patiently to one side, hat in hand.

Corrie looked wide-eyed at the waiting sailor.

Billy Brown.

Was she or wasn't she? How do you tell if somebody is a woman pretending to be a man? Was this the girl in the shanty?

'I shall charge you both for your Slops,' said the purser, looking over his nose-pinching eyeglasses at Corrie and Jim and making a careful note in his ledger before leaving the deck with his portmanteau back under his arm.

Corrie grinned at Jim.

The purser's words were both good and bad news. The bad news was that the purser would be docking some of their pay, while the good news was that, far from being punished for helping themselves to fresh clothes from the bin in the laundry, they were to be paid real money for their work as sailors from this day forward, and, if she remembered the *Table of Rates of Pay* correctly, they would receive no less than one pound, three shillings and sixpence a month each.

'Go and prove your worth,' said the master. 'Brown here will show you the ropes.'

Corrie did her best to calm her elation. She had hoodwinked the master and the purser. She, a girl, was now officially a member of the *Swift*'s male crew! It was too good to be true.

I had better not make any mistakes. I'll have to master a hundred small skills. I'll have to learn the correct way to address a petty officer, how to eat from a mess tin (she was very hungry and wondered when sailors had breakfast) how to stow her hammock (if anybody remembered to allot her a hammock) and she would have to accustom herself to sleeping four hours at a time, and being roused day and night to climb the rigging (which was scary) or to fight the French (even scarier).

She gnawed at her knuckles as she raised her eyes to the masts and yards high over her head.

She had never climbed masts as tall as these, nor fought in a battle, but now it seemed likely she would have to do both, and here was her mysterious trainer, Billy Brown, waiting for her.

Billy Brown was a Jamaican with large soulful eyes, lean, nimble, and sure-footed, with hair cropped short in ringlets, and small, elegant nut-brown hands and feet.

'Do you see that wooden thing that is halfway up the mainmast?' asked Billy Brown. 'That is what we call the maintop. You no see it?'

'We see it,' chorused Corrie and Jim.

'I be captain of maintop. Up you go to that platform. You, Corrie, you race your brother Jim. Go! I meet you there.'

Corrie looked at Jim. Many times they had raced one another along the shore of Quidi Vidi lake.

'One for sorrow, two for mirth, three for a wedding, and off we *go!*'

They ran in their bare feet, tearing across the freshly scrubbed white boards.

Corrie heard a sailor up in the maintop cry 'View Halloo!' That was the resounding cry of the fox hunter who spies a fox dashing across an open moor. She saw maintop men lean out over the platform rail to have a better look at the two newly pressed souls who were vying to be the first to reach their lofty platform in the sky.

Corrie ran as fast as she could, determined to do her best, and as she ran, she noticed that the sailors up in the maintop with their fox calls were not their only spectators. She saw, standing in the shade of the Well Deck, and half hidden by a jolly boat upended for caulking, none other than Augustus Sly. When she saw him gazing intently at her with his greedy little eyes, she put her tongue out at him.

She saw his eyes narrow. He went red in the face.

He's a pig. I hate him.

Jim ran like a hare and reached the small ropes

before Corrie did. He leapt from the deck into the tarry cordage, and Corrie began her own climb a second later, having been distracted by Sly, and so began her climb to the right of and slightly below her brother. What a climb it was! A hundred feet straight up, and the devil take the hindmost! It was maddening how the ropes sagged beneath her feet and hands. Jim's movements as he climbed twisted the ladder of ropes this way and that, making the ascent even more difficult.

As she mounted higher and higher, she became conscious of the great curve of the mainsail blotting out the sky – it was a sail larger than any she had seen – and she began to feel the ponderous gyrations of the *Swift* as she gamely met every swelling wave on her quarter and then smashed that billow into a tumbled confusion of froth and weed that trailed in her wake. What a splendid vessel she was! Corrie was delighted she had joined a ship that was the very epitome of the victory of mind over matter, a hymn to the ingenuity and resourcefulness of her designers, built to a modern design and equipped with modern instruments and meticulous charts to help her officers steer her clear of shoals.

Higher and higher Corrie went, until she was looking down on the sea like an eagle and the waves looked like the wrinkles on Mr. Weevil's face. She was doing her best to overtake her brother, but he was still ahead. She could see the planking of the maintop platform overhead now and those planks were looming closer with every heave of her arms and every push of her legs. She wiped sweat from her forehead. Was Jim going to beat her to the maintop? Was her brother going to win the race?

She looked about her urgently, searching for some other route that might allow her to arrive first and win. Jim was heading for the Lubbers' Hole, which was the easy way to attain the platform by climbing up though the opening cut out of the platform close to mast. But there was another more dangerous, faster way to reach the platform, if she could summon up enough courage to use it. She could climb the futtock shrouds. That was a shortcut, risky for a beginner.

She swung herself around, caught the nearest of the futtock shrouds, transferred her grip, and hung there like a monkey, upside down. She was surprised and relieved to find that it was much easier and faster to climb upside down, with her weight stretching the shrouds taut. When the moment came to put her foot on the maintop rail, a lean brown hand appeared out of nowhere to steady her and to help her keep her balance. She landed lightly on the platform deck.

'Billy Brown!' she said, amazed, gazing into the Jamaican's eyes. 'I thought I left you behind down on the deck. How did you get up here?'

Billy Brown grinned, exposing rows of pearly white teeth, and said 'The Dutty Duppy Man do it.'

Corrie helped her brother up though the Lubbers' Hole. 'Who is the Dutty Duppy Man?' she asked.

'You no see the Dutty Duppy Man?' said Brown. 'You maintop man now, and your brother he maintop man, too. All these men maintop men. All of them are my family. You are my family. Now the Dutty Duppy Man and I, we help you learn the lines. This is clew line. What this line do?'

Corrie followed the catenary curve of the line with her eye. 'It trusses up the clews at the bottom corners of the mainsail,' she answered.

Brown nodded, and put Corrie's hand on another line. 'All right. This be bunt line. What bunt line do?'

Again her eye followed the line to its seating in the foot of the great sail. 'It's a line for hauling up the foot of the sail for furling,' she said.

'Good,' said Brown. 'And this line over here?'

'A halyard for raising and lowering the sail,' said Jim quickly, not wanting to left out.

Corrie looked about her, trying to grasp the working of the maintop in its entirety. Handling the square sails of the *Swift* looked more complicated than handling the fore-and-aft rig of their uncle's schooner the *Maggie Rose*, but the principles were the same, and Jim knew those principles.

I stole Jim's thunder. I beat him in the race. I hope he's not mad at me.

'New maintop man must creep before him walk,' Brown cautioned, eyeing first Corrie and then Jim. 'New maintop men work together. You two work together?'

Corrie and Jim nodded.

'Take them up to the trussles, Billy,' said one of the maintop men. Another opened his mouth wide and waggled his tongue like a snake, making his fellow topmen laugh.

Corrie made a face. She felt a tingle of foreboding.

The Dutty Duppy Man has a snake's tongue. I hope I don't meet him.

Corrie craned her neck and looked up at the trestle-trees, two long pieces of timber fitted at the mast head in a fore-and-aft direction. They were far above her head, and that white spot way, way up there must be a seabird.

The bird opened its beak wide, uttered a long drawn-out call and eyed her with disdain from its lofty perch as if to say 'I dare you!'

'That gull he thinks we is scaredy-cats,' said Brown. 'Come. We show that gull who is the boss.'

Corrie felt Billy Brown's energy wash over her.

Is Billy Brown a woman? I am about to find out.

She followed Billy Brown into the heights.

VI

HOW do you tell if the person climbing ahead of you is a woman? Is there something about the way her hips move, or about the turn of her ankle?

She drinks rum and chews tobacco.
Spend my money on Billy Brown.

Yes, Brown could very well be a woman.
Does she know that I am a woman?
Corrie had to wonder why Brown was leading her up to the highest part of the vessel. Was it to test their mettle? To see if they would flinch? She glanced at the deck far below and then wished she hadn't looked down. People far below her looked like heads with legs. Those tiny figures must be the lieutenant keeping watch, and the master at the binnacle. Those blobs of white by the taffrail must be Norah and the White Lady. As she ventured higher she felt the mainmast top to which she clung move in ever widening arcs, magnifying the *Swift*'s rhythmic motions up and down, forward and aft, and to port and starboard. Corrie looked up over Billy Brown's shoulder at the cheeky gull up in the cross trees and saw that the bird was much closer now, and was stretching its wings preparatory to flight. She could see its angry yellow eye glaring at her. With a scream of defiance the creature took to the air, floated effortlessly on the wind for a moment, regarding them with scorn, and then soared away and down to join other gulls that were swooping

in the ship's wake.

'Gull gone,' said Billy Brown. 'We take his place. You give me hand.'

Corrie was not sure she wanted to let go of the rope, but she did.

Why do I trust you, Billy Brown? But I do. I trust you with my life.

Billy Brown's small brown hand felt warm, firm, and callused.

'Up we go,' said Billy Brown, and hauled Corrie and her brother up one at a time to stand beside her, and there they balanced on the soles of their bare feet on the crosstree timbers like three high-wire performers amusing a circus crowd under a big top. The timbers on which they stood continued to describe their lazy circles in the sky while the wind ruffled Corrie's hair and threatened to dislodge her hat.

The three stood there in silence for a while, their hands holding the flag halyards. They gazed about at the wide horizon, taking in the vast spaces of the world. There was no sign of land.

I am safe. The wetness cannot come up here. All that awful water cannot get me. I float here high above the sea of horrors. I look down on my vanquished enemy from far, far above.

'Wahooo!' shouted Jim. He was elated.

Corrie looked down at the watchers on the deck below to see if her brother's shout would provoke a reaction, but saw none. They had not heard him. They were that high up.

'Up here in the trussles,' said Billy Brown quietly,

'be good place talk, nobody hear.'

'Why did you choose my brother and me to be maintop men?' asked Corrie quickly. It was not the question she really wanted to ask. What she was dying to know was: Is she or isn't he?

Are you a woman, Billy Brown?

Corrie was not quite ready to ask that bold question straight out, for she did not want to be rude.

Billy Brown must have guessed where Corrie's question was leading, for she replied: 'Norah in the laundry she spy on you. *That Corrie Harriman she is a girl*, she say to Mrs. Keeper.'

'The White Lady is Mrs. Keeper?'

'The White Lady she is Mrs. Anne Keeper, wife of First Lieutenant. Very important lady. Mrs. Keeper she keep things under that big hat of hers. She send her boy to maintop with message for Billy. Message say: Billy, you make these two young people maintop men. You look after this young woman Corrie. You keep this young woman Corrie away from that creature of Babylon, that bad man the master-at-arms.'

'The master-at-arms threw us in the bilge hole last night,' said Corrie, 'and in the inn he told that crony of his, Foster, to hit my brother on the head. I hate them both. But why did Mrs. Keeper ask you to look after me? How can *you* keep us safe?'

Billy Brown smiled, exposing her fine strong white teeth. 'All fruits ripe,' she said.

Corrie took a deep breath and then asked the question she had not dared to ask before: 'Are you a woman, Billy Brown?'

'I be able seaman,' Billy Brown replied carefully, and threw Corrie a shrewd look as if to say 'Go on, girl. Figure it out.'

Corrie returned Billy Brown's frank look with one of her own. 'I heard the sailors singing about you,' she said. 'They called you *she*. That's why Mrs. Keeper sent her boy to you, wasn't it? Because you're a woman.'

'As an able seaman,' said Billy Brown, 'I am paid one pound, nine shillings and sixpence a month. I got family need their dinner pig. Men they get paid. Women they do not get paid. So it's Mister Billy Brown to you, and no more chatty-chatty, Mister Corrie Harriman.'

'I won't say a word, Billy,' said Corrie. 'I *knew* there had to be women serving in the navy. I just *knew* it.' She grinned happily at Billy Brown, and Billy grinned back, her bright teeth gleaming in the sun, and the wind teasing at her hair.

Then Billy Brown stopped smiling and she said 'If that Augustus Sly give you any more trouble, you tell Billy. We make plenty trouble for that one. You maintop man now, you and your brother. All maintop men one big family. We look after our own.'

'Mrs. Keeper will tell her husband about me,' said Corrie, 'and the first lieutenant will tell the captain.'

'No problem,' Billy Brown replied. 'The captain know all about me. Part of captain's job know all about everybody, and to keep what he knows to himself. No worry, everything cook and curry. You work hard, you do what Billy says, one day you be captain of the maintop.'

'I really can have a career in the navy,' said Corrie. 'Do you hear that, Jim?'

'I hear,' her brother replied. 'But that child who carried the message about you won't be keeping your secret, so it won't be long before Sly hears about it, and he'll find a way to stop your pay. He'll force the captain's hand.'

'You don't *want* me to be a sailor,' said Corrie, disappointed in her brother.

Jim stared at the distant horizon. 'I think it's going to be very hard for you, pretending all the time. You'll have to work twice as hard as a man just to prove you can do a man's work.'

'You no done yet, Jim Harriman?' asked Billy Brown, frowning. 'Why you down-press your sister? You maintop men, you two Harrimans, you ready to do what Billy say right now?'

'Yes, sir,' said Corrie, wondering what new challenge was coming, and bracing herself for the worst.

'Yes, sir,' echoed Jim.

'I wants you two maintop men to climb all the way down to the deck with your eyes shut.'

'Are you serious?' said Corrie. 'We must be two hundred feet above the sea.'

'You listen to Billy. One of these days you maintop men have to go all the way down on a dark night with no moon, no stars, and maybe you is in a big trouble, with the storm wind a-blowing, whooo, and the French guns a-firing, boom-boom, and you got to go along about your business. You make sail, then how you get back down to the deck? Move your backsides. All the way down in the dark. Close your eyes this minute and down you go, Corrie Harriman.'

'You're serious?' said Corrie, hoping this was a joke.

'Yes, I be serious. I be all-the-way-down serious. Look at that brother of yours. He start down already. You want he leave you behind? Feel your way down, girl, feel your way down with your fingers and toes.'

'Right,' said Corrie, and she closed her eyes tight shut, made an effort of will, and started down.

As she descended she became more aware than ever of the rigging singing in the wind, and she felt the cords beneath her hands tighten and droop with every swoop and shudder of the ship. The morning breeze tickled the soles of her bare feet as she felt about with her toes for the next line down. Having her eyes closed made her pay attention to the sun-warmed tarry smell of the cordage, and the pong of the rancid goose grease that lubricated the sheave wheels inside the blocks. As she lowered herself from cord to cord, she became uncertain of how far she had come and how much further she had to go, and was sorely tempted to take a peek, but perhaps that was something a boy would not do. Perhaps a boy would keep his eyes tightly shut until the moment he stepped onto the deck.

The lower I go, the nearer I am to the water.

She felt something new beneath her foot. Planking. Not the deck, not yet. She had arrived back at the maintop. She groped about for the maintop rail, found it, *thank goodness*, and then followed the rail along, hand over hand, and lowered herself gingerly down the hole in the platform. The ratlines were shorter here, barely long enough to hang onto, but she fumbled her way down nevertheless, and vowed to repeat this drill until she could picture every cord and every sheet, and find them, if need be, in fog or in gun smoke.

The water is nearer now. I hear it. I feel the spray on my cheek. I am the girl sailor who is frightened of the sea. That's me. I must not let Jim see how terrified I am.

Down Corrie went, the lines growing wider by degrees, until at last her toes felt the true deck, and she opened her eyes and there was Jim waiting patiently for her.

'Don't look behind you,' he said quietly. 'Sly is watching us from the forecastle.'

'I don't know about you,' said Corrie, 'but I'm starving. When did we last eat? I keep thinking of Bessie's lamb's tails at the inn.'

'Something does smell good,' said Jim, sniffing the air. Tempting aromas from the ship's galley were wafting in his direction.

Drawn by the appetizing vapors, Corrie and Jim made their way to the waist and discovered that it was there in the ship's midriff that they messed with their fellow maintop men. They sat on their haunches to eat their rations. Corrie shoveled parboiled peas and stewed beef from her meal pan into her mouth with the help of a piece of hard ship's biscuit baked long ago in the St. John's victualing yard. As she enjoyed her long-awaited meal, she watched the officers on the quarterdeck. She could see that they were taking their noon sights. The master, old Mr. Weevil, was the first to shoot the sun. She watched him peer through the telescope of his sextant, and then swing the index bar along the arc scale. Corrie had handled her uncle's sextant and so she knew what Mr. Weevil would be seeing in the horizon mirror: the disc of the sun and the horizon superimposed one upon the other. She watched him adjust the Gascoigne screw and squeeze the clamp. He made his sighting. He took the sextant from his eye and tipped the instrument sideways on its side to show his reading to the purser, Mr. Hartnell, who had brought along quill and paper. She saw Mr. Hartnell peer through the magnifying glass and heard him say '*Hopes springs eternal in the human breast*, Mr. Weevil, perhaps you have your numbers right today.'

The master was not amused by Mr. Hartnell and his poetry. 'Make a note of the figure, you fool. You are keeping the captain waiting.'

The captain?

Corrie craned her neck. She had yet to lay eyes on the commander of the *Swift*, and was anxious to see what kind of a man he was. She saw Mr. Weevil pass the instrument to a younger man, clean shaven, bareheaded, and dressed in a smart dark blue uniform jacket with epaulettes of bullion, a cream waistcoat with gold buttons, and cream tight-fitting trousers tucked into knee length boots of dark polished leather.

She heard the captain say 'Thank you, Mr. Weevil' and watched him put his eye to the instrument.

The curly-haired midshipman stepped up to the ship's bell and rang it. *Ting-ting, ting-ting, ting-ting, ting-ting.* Eight bells. Noon. That was exactly the right moment to measure the height of the sun above the horizon.

The captain made a fine adjustment and then said something to the purser, who scratched away with his quill. Then the captain released the clamp, and handed the sextant to the midshipman who had just rung the bell. 'Let's see what you can do, Mr. Potts.'

At this the midshipman looked nervous. Corrie watched him take the instrument from the captain, put the telescope to his eye, and fiddle with the index bar. Corrie could see how hard young Potts found it to bring the image of the sun down to the horizon. His hands shook. She sympathized. It had to be difficult to take a good reading under the watchful eyes of your master *and* your captain. Part of her wanted to rush over and help the boy, but she knew she could do no such thing. She and her brother had made fools of themselves on the quarterdeck earlier. She dared not risk further rebuke.

Potts read the arc scale and gave the purser his reading.

'You have done your worst, Potts,' said the purser, raising one eyebrow. 'But *the plaintive numbers flow for old, unhappy, far-off things.* With a reading like this one, Mr. Potts, I am sure our ship is marooned upon the peaks of Himalaya.'

Potts blushed and passed the sextant back to the master, who laid the device in a velvet-lined wooden case, closed the lid, engaged the fasteners and walked off with the box.

Corrie hunkered back down to shovel some more food into her mouth. She decided she liked Potts. She wished she, herself, were a midshipman instead of an ordinary seamen. As a midshipman, she could have shown Potts how to keep the disk of the sun steady on the horizon and how to clamp the index bar gently. She liked Potts's smile and the way the sun lit up his hair. But she was not a midshipman, she was just a maintop man, working under Billy Brown to handle the sails, and had quite enough on her plate for the moment without dreaming about Mr. Potts.

She was pleased to discover that the navy fed sailors generously. The food was hot and filled her stomach. As Corrie crunched up the last of her biscuit, and watched Billy Brown chat easily with her other maintop men, it came to her in a flash of understanding that they all knew Billy Brown was a woman, and they all treated her with respect. They all *liked* Billy Brown. Corrie decided that she liked Billy Brown, too, and wondered how Billy Brown had come to serve on the *Swift*, and how many years she had been in the navy. Captain of the Maintop was an important job. How droll that Billy had to depend on the silence of her fellow sailors to draw her monthly pay, and that she, Corrie, now found herself in the same boat.

Quite apart from being paid, Corrie was thrilled that there were prospects in the navy for adventurous women who were not afraid to dress like men and to act like men, and that filled her with hope, but on the other hand she was not sure she knew how to get along with her shipmates in the easy give-and-take way that Billy did.

Corrie felt happy, all the same. She felt at home in the *Swift*.

Someone snatched her stew pan rudely from her hands.

Startled, she raised her eyes.

The master-at-arms, Augustus Sly, stood before her glaring, his fat cheeks suffused with crimson. When he spoke she smelled his cheesy breath.

'You've got a nerve, you have, Harriman,' he said. 'You think I don't know who and what you are?'

Corrie rose to her feet. 'That's my dinner, Mr. Sly,' she said, tilting her chin and looking him in the eye. 'Give it back.'

'Give it back? Give it back?' The master-at-arms mocked her. 'How about I shove it in your pretty face?'

Out of the corner of her eye, Corrie saw Jim lay down his own dinner pan and stand up, his fists clenched. She saw his knuckles turn white. She heard her brother say 'Back off, Sly. You haven't got your bully-boy with you today.'

'You can't talk to a warrant officer like that,' said Sly. 'I'm the master-at-arms. You lay a finger on me, and I'll have you up before the captain.'

Billy Brown stepped in. 'You leave my topmen be, Mr. Sly, or the master he is going to hear what you is up to in the dog watches. You better take care. When chicken is merry, hawk is near.'

'Stay out of this, Brown,' said Sly, swinging

around. 'This is between me and Corrie here. What kind of a name is that, anyway? Doesn't sound like a *boy's* name.'

Corrie's hopes for the future were being dashed before her eyes.

This worthless, bullying policeman is going to tell them who I really am.

VII

BILLY Brown said 'Why you got it in for this man, Sly? You no done yet? You put this man in the bilge hole, now you take away this man dinner? You give Ordinary Seaman Harriman back his pan. You do that this minute, or I tell Mister Weevil about them games you is playing and those bones you is playing with that come up sixes … all … the … time?'

The topmen on the Well Deck laughed and rattled their dinner pans.

'Don't you make fun of me, Brown. I'm Augustus Sly. I'm the master-at-arms. I don't have to take no lip from you. I'll have you on the gratings.'

A murmur of anger arose from the men on the well deck. By threatening to have the captain of the maintop hauled before the ship's captain and flogged, Sly had overstepped the bounds of his authority, and the maintop men knew it. A dozen sailors laid down their dinner pans and rose silently to their feet. Their faces were impassive. They stood there and they looked at the master-at-arms, and said not a word. They did not have to speak. Their intent was clear. They were going to beat the living daylights out of Augustus Sly.

Sly's eyes flicked from sailor to sailor. The blood left his cheeks.

Corrie watched Sly racking his brains. He could call on the marines to arrest the lot of them, but that would mean upsetting the master and the captain, and there would be bound to be some kind of an inquiry, and when all came out into the open, the captain might indeed put an end to Sly's highly lucrative lower deck gambling operation.

'Just a little joke between friends,' said the master-at-arms, who had never told a joke in his life.

Slowly, carefully, the master-at-arms backed away from the threatening crowd with Corrie's stew pan still in his hand.

'Give Harriman back his dinner, Mr. Sly,' said Billy Brown.

'Here you are, Harriman,' said Sly, returning the pan to her hands reluctantly. What he really wanted to do was throw her dinner in her face. 'Don't you talk back at me like that again, you hear? I knows all about you, see? *All* about you.'

Corrie got the message.

So that's it. Somebody has told him I am a girl, and so he believes he can take advantage of me. The man is crass and uncouth. He'd better not try anything. I'll make him regret it if he does.

Corrie took back the pan. She did not thank Sly, having no wish to dignify his ignominious retreat. She looked him directly in the eye, broadcasting contempt. Sly was a dangerous fool who should never have been appointed the ship's policeman, and something would have to be done about him.

'Cheeky little bitch,' said Sly, and he spat on the deck, turned on his heel and walked away.

The men who had stood up to support Corrie hunkered down again to get on with their meal, and resumed their conversations.

'You no mind that Sly,' said Billy Brown quietly.

'The higher a monkey climbs, the more he exposes.'

Corrie was trying to figure out what Billy meant by that when a shout came from aloft.

'Strange sail! Strange sail off the larboard bow!'

Corrie and her fellow sailors bolted down the last of the stew, rinsed their pans under the wash pump, stowed them in the galley, and ran up the ratlines to the maintop platform to take a look.

Corrie shaded her eyes and peered at the distant horizon. Yes, a vessel was just discernible. She was hull down but her sails were visible.

'Her sails look pale,' whispered Corrie to her brother.

'Yes,' said Jim. English sails tended to be darkened by years of service, but the sails on this stranger looked bright, as if fresh from the sailcloth factory in Toulon. 'She's making a run for Saint Pierre.'

There came a dull, flat report, and Corrie spied a puff of smoke that left the stranger's side and drifted slowly away on the wind. Her heart raced. It was the first time she had heard a gun fired at sea. The strange sail is French, she thought. She has seen us. She has fired a gun to alert the Frenchmen on the islands of the presence of a British warship. 'Her shape is changing,' she remarked. 'She is coming about.'

Billy Brown made a speaking trumpet of her hands and called down to the deck below. 'The strange sail has hauled her wind, captain.'

'Thank you, Billy,' the captain replied.

Looking down from the rail, Corrie saw Captain Redburn's cheerful, intelligent face looking up at her.

I wonder if he knows I'm a woman. If he doesn't know now, he's bound to find out soon.

The ship's captain embodied something of the King's majesty and not a little of the King's royal authority, and there was, in the minds of many aboard, an aura that set Captain Redburn apart from ordinary mortals. The captain exuded a sense of presence not shared by his fellow luminary the pompous Mr. Weevil, the ship's master, nor by the wry and well-read Mr. Hartnell, the ship's purser, who went round reciting poetry at everyone.

'Break out the gallants,' the captain said in a deep and carrying voice fit to better a storm.

Corrie was galvanized into action.

Breaking out the topgallants is my job! I'm a maintop man!

She leapt into the shrouds and climbed up the ratlines as fast as she could. This is no drill, she told herself. This is the real thing. There is an enemy ship in sight, and now it is up to me, my brother and ten other far more experienced maintop men to run out along the main topgallant yard and loose the gaskets. The *Swift* must make more sail if she is to live up to her name and catch that enemy ship before she delivers her supplies to Saint-Pierre.

Other seamen were letting go the clewlines and buntlines, and making ready to haul on the sheets to shape the sail to catch the wind, but before they could haul away she and her fellow top men must undo the tiers and let the sail fall.

Here was the topgallant yard. She was the first to

reach it and so had the furthest to run to reach the end of the yardarm. She ignored the footropes suspended beneath the yard and dashed out along the top of the timber. She felt like a high-wire performer in a circus. Her bare feet felt where the top edge of the sail was bent on. Out of breath, she came to the end of the yard.

God knows how many feet I am above the deck right now. I must try not to look.

She threw herself chest down on the yard end and felt about with her feet for the Flemish horse. Got it! That was better. It felt good to have something to take her weight. Now she had to let go of the gasket and free the line used to hold the stowed sail in place.

She saw that somebody had secured the sail with a round turn and two half hitches. Her fingers made short work of the knot.

The sailor beside her was not so handy. 'Come on, you brute of a tier!' he cried in desperation, and he pushed and pulled without making any progress.

'Campbell, is that you?'

'They'll tie me to the gratings for this. That's what they do with dunderheads.'

'I'll help you,' said Corrie and wriggled along the yard until she could reach his gasket. 'You have to tease the end out first like this.' She freed the knot.

'I'm much obliged,' said Campbell.

With the last of the gaskets freed, the bulk of the sail fell away from the yard with a mighty thundering and flapping of canvas.

The sheets were hauled tight, and Corrie felt the *Swift* leap forwards like a startled horse, spurred on by the wind in her straining gallants.

The topmast tipped alarmingly to port. The rigging began to hum on a higher note.

'I should have done it myself,' said Campbell.

'You're learning,' said Corrie.

Campbell sighed. 'I'm a choob.'

'We're flying!' cried her brother Jim, and he waved at Corrie from further down the yard.

'Take your time,' cautioned Billy Brown from the other end of the yard. 'Come on back down with Billy. Slowly does it.'

They obeyed Billy Brown's order and made their way back along the yard and down the ratlines to the maintop.

Corrie found the wooden platform strangely calm and peaceful after her exertions in the heights. She leaned on the maintop rail, and was astonished to find herself face to face and at close quarters with Captain Redburn, who had climbed up to join them. Without thinking she put out a hand to help the captain make the transfer from the futtocks to the platform.

His hand feels smooth and strong.

'Thank you,' said the captain, swinging his legs over the rail and landing lightly on his polished boots. He straightened his uniform coat, adjusted the sword at his waist, and took a spyglass from his coat pocket. Before he put the glass to his eye he paused and looked Corrie over. 'You must be new. I don't recall your face.'

'Corrie Harriman, sir. Ordinary seaman. Pressed in St. John's, sir.'

'Well, Corrie Harriman, what do you make of this Frenchman?' he asked, putting the glass to his eye.

'Supply ship, sir, for the French garrison at Saint-Pierre,' said Corrie, shading her eyes to take a better look at the enemy. 'She won't make the harbor on this tack, and she daren't go about for fear we shall overtake her.'

'You know too much for an ordinary seaman, Harriman,' said the captain, continuing to study his enemy through his glass. 'I think you are a French spy. One of Jean-Pierre Troude's people, perhaps?'

'No, sir,' said Corrie, shocked at the captain's accusation. 'Just an ordinary seaman, sir.'

'You signed the muster book yourself,' the captain replied. 'Not many ordinary seamen know how to do that, and there's something odd about your handwriting, the purser tells me, and my master-at-arms says you are not to be trusted. So. You have only been in my ship for a few hours and already you have given us cause for concern. What is your advice for your captain, mister Spy? Do we engage this supply ship or not?'

'Not in daylight, sir. She'll put her hook down now and then rely on the big guns of Saint-Pierre to frighten us off.'

'How do you know they have big guns at Saint-Pierre?'

'My father told me, sir. After Vice-Admiral Richery and his squadron drove the English out of the islands and sank their ships, Richery left a contingent on Saint Pierre, enough men to work the battery, so my father assured me. Look there! Our chase is coming up into the wind.'

'So she is,' said the captain, adjusting his glass. 'How much does Troude pay you?'

'I've never heard of anyone called Troude, sir.'

Puffs of smoke appeared in the embrasures of the bastions of Saint-Pierre, and, moments later, thunderous concussions split the air. Something went flying past Corrie's head screaming like a banshee and the main backstay parted with a deep reverberating sound like the plucking of a giant harp string. Corrie felt the mast shudder. Six columns of white water fountained up unexpectedly from the seas off the starboard bow.

'If you are not working for Troude, then perhaps you are one of Richery's people, planted in my crew to deceive me,' said the captain.

'Eight hundred yards?' said Corrie out loud, doing her best to judge the distance by the fall of the shot. This was her first battle. She had to learn to judge distances.

The captain lowered his spyglass and looked directly at her.

Corrie felt his presence.

He has blue eyes, and a cleft in his chin.

'Nearer a thousand yards,' said Redburn. 'Your first voyage?'

Corrie stared at him. 'Permission to ask a question?' she ventured, very conscious that this was the captain she was talking to, and that he could have her punished for her impertinence if she overstepped the bounds of polite conversation.

'Go ahead,' said the captain, still looking her straight in the face.

Corrie gathered her strength.

I'll tell him what I'm thinking. I'll be bold, and risk everything, even though it is not really my place to speak.

She blurted out 'The enemy is putting down a kedge. He may try to slip and run in the morning. If you plan to bring the *Swift* back tonight, under cover of darkness, before the moon rises, and you wish to keep out of range of the fort while sending in the boats to cut her out, then how will you be able to tell how far from the shore we are? In the dark? Sir?'

The captain regarded her curiously as if she were some insect that had crawled out of the woodwork of his ship. 'I have a man in the chains casting the lead at present, and I shall have that same man casting the lead tonight.'

'The lead is armed?' asked Corrie.

'Soft shell in five fathoms,' replied the captain. 'We should have no trouble feeling our way back in, providing that the weather holds. Well, now, Mr. Spy, now that you know what I plan to do, how are you going to signal my intentions to the captain of that supply ship?'

'I'm not a spy, sir, and I'm not going to signal anybody,' said Corrie.

'You know a far too much about the navy,' said the captain. 'You cannot blame me for being suspicious.'

Corrie grinned. 'My father, Archibald Harriman, is a lieutenant in the *Queen Charlotte*, sir. At least, my brother and I think he is still in the *Queen Charlotte*.'

'Then you'll be sorry to hear,' said the captain, suddenly looking serious, 'that the *Queen Charlotte* caught fire off the island of Cabrera and blew up three months ago. Many officers and men died in the accident. It was in the *Gazette*.'

Corrie froze. She went as white as a sheet.

It can't be true. Not Daddy. I feel sick.

She cast a look at Jim. His face, too, had gone white.

'Who's this?' asked the captain, looking from one to the other. 'Another of Troude's agents?'

'My brother, sir,' said Corrie.

The captain closed his spyglass with a snap, and turned to Billy Brown.

'Billy, are these two Harrimans ready for action?'

Billy Brown made a show of looking Corrie and Jim over carefully. 'If the Dutty Duppy man come, he feed them to the Houngan,' she said.

'Four fathom,' shouted the sailor casting the lead down in the chains. 'Black shell.'

The guns of the fort bellowed again, louder and closer this time. Fresh columns of water sprang up, and this time the shots plunged into the sea off the port bow.

'They'll soon have our range,' said the captain. He stepped to the rail and shouted to the helmsman down on the quarterdeck. 'Let her fall away, Jensen. We've seen all we need to see.'

'Aye aye, captain,' said the Mikkel Jensen. 'Let her fall away.' The man at the helm spun the wheel, and sea and coast changed places as the *Swift* turned from the island and stood out into the gulf.

'We leave with our tail between our legs. We let our enemy see us vanish over the horizon. We hope to lull him into a false sense of security.' The captain put his glass back in his pocket, puffed out his cheeks and exhaled slowly. 'Report to me in ten minutes in my cabin, Corrie Harriman, and bring that brother of yours with you.'

'Aye aye, sir,' said Corrie.

Captain Redburn swung himself into the shrouds. 'Billy,' he said, 'do something about that backstay.'

'Right away, sir,' said Billy Brown.

As soon as the captain had left the maintop, Billy Brown gave Corrie an elbow in the ribs. 'Move your backsides, you Harrimans. You heard the captain. His cabin. Ten minutes. Go smarten up! You look like you just begin for dead.'

Corrie and Jim, both pale with shock, left the maintop in a hurry.

VIII

AS Corrie made her way down to the deck, she thought about the devastating news concerning their father's ship.

If the *Queen Charlotte* had been destroyed last March and so many of her people killed, what had happened to her father? Had Dad been in the ship at the time? Had he died along with his shipmates? It was too awful to think about. Part of her refused to believe Dad was gone, and that she would never see him again, while another part of her feared to learn the truth. Was there some way to find out what had really happened? Would somebody at the Admiralty know?

Why did Redburn want to talk to her brother and herself in his cabin? Did he really think they were spying for the French? If the French had spies in English crews, were there English spies aboard that French supply ship sheltering under the guns of the fort? Might she end up fighting one of her own people by mistake?

Corrie gulped. She might soon be involved in hand-to-hand combat. What did she know of real fighting? Nothing.

My fencing master told me how to thrust and parry, but I don't suppose they'll give me an épée to fight with should we board this Frenchman. A flying parry or a riposte may be uncalled for if all I have to fight with is a belaying pin.

She had noticed a fierce look in the captain's eyes when he spoke of Jean-Pierre Troude and of Vice-

Admiral Richery. Richery she knew about, but who was Jean-Pierre Troude? Had Redburn and Troude met one another at some diplomatic reception in a neutral port? Meetings between officers on both sides of this war were not uncommon. Had Troude challenged him?

Corrie checked her tumbling thoughts and forced herself to focus on the immediate question:

Why does the captain want to see Jim and me right now?

Corrie and her brother returned to the laundry to scrub the tar off their hands with the help of a few drops of lemon juice supplied by Gladys. They even tried to comb the wind-tangles from their hair with an ivory comb of Norah's.

'Thanks,' said Corrie, handing back the comb.

All spruced up, they made their way aft along the upper deck, climbed up the companion stairs to the quarterdeck, walked past the mizzen mast, and came in trepidation to the door of the captain's cabin.

The door was guarded by that stalwart but slow-thinking marine, Sergeant Deering.

'Wot are you two up to this time?' said the sergeant, regarding them suspiciously.

'Captain wants to see us,' said Corrie.

'Why would any captain want to see a pair of no-good sailors like you?'

'He just said we were to come,' said Jim. 'He didn't say why.'

Sergeant Deering's ape-like brow furrowed and his tiny eyes narrowed. 'If you're having me on…' he said slowly.

Corrie felt sorry for Sergeant Deering. She sensed that many things lay outside this sergeant's experience. Anything at all unusual, like the captain wanting to talk to a couple of ordinary seamen, seemed to fill the poor man with apprehension. Perhaps Sergeant Deering was dimly aware of some of his own limitations, and constantly worried that others might discover his failings. Although it was not her place to do so, Corrie decided to put the man at ease by giving him a direct order.

'Knock on the door and tell the captain we are here,' she said.

To her surprise, the marine did exactly as she told him. He knocked on the captain's door. 'This better not be a trick,' he whispered to Corrie.

'It's not,' she whispered back.

'What is it?' said the captain's voice.

'Them two boys what joined Billy Brown in the maintop, is here, and they says as how you ordered them to report, sir.'

'Show them in.'

The marine opened the door and came to attention.

Corrie and Jim walked past the marine and into the captain's cabin, keeping their heads down as they did so, for the beams were as low here as on the gun deck. The marine closed the door behind them, and they were alone with the captain.

Corrie, worried as she was, was filled with a solemn joy. She had entered a sanctuary.

I'm in the captain's cabin. I can tell what sort of person our captain is by the way he keeps his cabin.

Through the stern windows she saw the *Swift*'s wake twinkling with sun stars. An upholstered window seat was strewn with charts. In a becket she spied a bevy of books bound in leather, their titles picked out in gilt: *A Journal of the Late and Important Blockade and Siege of Gibraltar by Samuel Ancel,* and *Brindley's Theatre of the Present War.* There were astronomical tables and manuals of seamanship and gunnery. Corrie stared greedily at the captain's library. There was so much she had to learn. She wanted to read every volume.

Both sides of the cabin contained a black cast iron gun mounted on a wooden carriage. Balls, chain shot and canisters lay in lockers, while the rammer, pricker and sponge were stowed in racks overhead.

Where does Captain Redburn sleep? I wonder what kind of a bed he has?

One end of the captain's bunk was just visible through an open doorway that led to his sleeping cabin. It was a mess. Somebody should have made up the captain's bunk bed. That servant of his, Harbottle, should have done that for him.

Here in the main cabin there were more lockers, one serving as a table, but no chairs.

Captain Redburn rummaged about among the papers on the window seat and came up with a copy of *Mottley's Naval and Military Journal.*

'I understand you can both read,' he said, and laid the article before them on the table. It was an account of 'The Loss of the Queen Charlotte.'

Corrie stared with growing horror at the printed

words.

'*The loss of his Majesty's ship Queen Charlotte, of 110 guns, Captain Todd, bearing the flag of Vice-Admiral Lord Keith, which took fire off the harbor of Leghorn, on the seventeenth of March 1800, and afterwards blew up, is distressing in the highest degree, and painful to relate,*' the account began, inauspiciously, and then went on to say that '*Lord Keith and some of the Officers were providentially on shore at Leghorn when the dreadful accident occurred.*'

Captain Redburn stripped off his uniform coat and laid it down on the window seat. 'Some cussed fool set fire to the straw in the stable. It may have been a French spy that started the blaze. The survivors are listed at the end of the report. You will find one name among them that may be of interest to you.'

Corrie turned to the end of the report and scanned the list of survivors anxiously. She read aloud the name of 'Lieutenant Archibald Harriman.'

She felt a burst of hope. Archibald was their father's name! Perhaps he had been ashore when his ship had caught fire.

'That's our Dad,' said Jim, relief showing on his face. 'He must be still alive.'

'I'm sorry if I frightened you,' said the captain. 'Perhaps, after all, you are not spies.'

Corrie stared at the captain. 'You really thought we were?'

'You've heard me speak of Troude,' said the captain.

'Is he the Frigate Captain in the *Tonnerre*?' asked

Corrie, recalling a conversation she had overheard in the Crown and Anchor.

'How do you know that name?' said the captain sharply.

'I heard fishermen talking in the pub, sir. Said they saw a big ship flying the flag of revolutionary France in a fog off Grand Manan, and read the name off her transom. They said she was called the Ton-Air. They were wondering what that name meant, and I told them it meant thunder, sir. Our governess taught us a little French, sir.'

'I'm glad she did,' said the captain. He pushed some of his charts aside and sat down on the window seat. 'We are going into action tonight. Have you seen action before?'

Corrie and Jim shook their heads.

'I have a task for you, Corrie. Can you man the yards of a strange ship in the middle of the night? There may not be any footropes. No doubt the French will take those in, or slacken them off and let them dangle down, in expectation of an attack.'

Corrie lifted her chin. 'Yes, sir. You can rely on me,' she said. She regarded Captain Redburn levelly. It must be hard being a captain, she thought, having to think of so many things at all at once.

'Yellow sand and black shell,' murmured the captain to himself, picking up a chart. He stood up, keeping his head down, and spread the chart on the table for their inspection, placing two pigs of ballast iron at the ends to keep the chart from rolling up again.

By the glow of the hanging lantern, Corrie peered

down at a host of spiny numbers that indicated the depths of the sea bottom. In her mind's eye she followed the rise and fall of the submarine vales and peaks that culminated in the islands of Saint-Pierre and Miquelon. She read with interest the notes to mariners: *beware the devil's teeth,* and *here be shoals at low tide.* Among the crowded numerals she saw careful descriptions of the sea bottom: *mud and shale* in one spot, *yellow sand with pebbles* in another, and, then, about a mile of shore: *yellow sand and black shell.*

'You are taking us in to here, sir?' she asked, tracing with her forefinger the limit of the black shell, a mile or so from the coast.

'Closer,' replied the captain. 'It's growing dark already. We'll be there soon. Go and blacken your faces. Corrie, you'll be with Billy Brown. Jim, your task will be to lower the supply ship's flag. Can I rely on you? The outcome of the fight may depend on that tricolor coming down.'

Jim was delighted. At last he had a real job to do, and his captain was taking him seriously. There was no more talk of spies. 'Yes, sir,' he said, happily.

Corrie wanted to sing for joy, but this was hardly the place to dance their hornpipe and butt their heads.

He's letting us both join the cutting out expedition. I feel a blaze of excitement. We must not let him down.

'Report to the master-at-arms, the pair of you, and he'll help you choose your weapons. I shall be on deck to inspect you shortly. Go!'

They left the captain's cabin in a hurry. They found Sly in the waist handing out dirks and cutlasses, and took their place, last in the queue.

When their turn came, Sly looked at them with contempt.

'No weapons for maintop men. You don't need them. You're just a bunch of monkeys. You won't be doing any fighting.'

'Captain told us to report here for arms,' said Jim. 'My job is to haul down the enemy flag. I shall be on deck, not in the rigging. I need a cutlass.'

'A cutlass, he says. A cutlass. La-de-da! Well, Harrison, I might just have a weapon here for you,' said Sly, rummaging in the arms chest. 'Yes, indeed I do. You're in luck, you are. This is the last cutlass left in the chest. Here you are.'

Jim took the weapon, buckled the sword belt around his waist and drew the blade from its scabbard. He tried the weight of the weapon with a few practice swings. 'It's falling apart. The guard is not attached to the stock properly,' he complained.

Sly narrowed his horrible little eyes. 'The first Frenchman you see will be the last. It won't matter what kind of weapon you've got, Harriman. You'll be run through, that's what. You'll be lying there on the deck of that foreign ship, bleeding to death. You won't get nowhere near that flag halyard to bring down that flag. How did you get out of that bilge hole? How'd you move that cask?'

'Still trying to figure that out, are you, Sly? I've a mind to try out this useless cutlass right now.'

'Don't you threaten me, you miserable rat's breakfast.'

MIDSHIPMAN HARRIMAN

'When you two have finished,' said Corrie, elbowing her brother to one side. 'I need a knife with a sheath in case I have to cut lanyards, and a belt. I'll wear the sheath at my waist,' said Corrie.

Sly pretended to look inside the arms chest. 'No knife for you. We're all out of knives. Maybe that Billy Brown will lend you one. Next time I comes looking for a bit of your dinner, you'd better be more polite to your master-at-arms.'

'I'll find a knife somewhere, Sly, and when I do, I hope I run into you,' said Corrie.

'I looks forward to that, I really do,' said Sly. 'You saucy girl.'

Corrie and Jim turned their backs on the despicable master-at-arms, and made their way hurriedly to the boat deck.

'I don't understand,' Jim whispered, minutes later, as they stood in line to be inspected. 'Why has Sly given me this battered old cutlass? Just look at this guard.'

'Sly doesn't like you,' Corrie whispered back. 'You escaped from his bilge hole, and now you're working for Billy Brown. But I shouldn't worry, your job is to find the enemy's flag halyard. With any luck you won't need the cutlass.'

'I'd better not need it. The wretched thing is coming to pieces.'

'Mr. Keeper,' said the captain, moving along the inspection line. 'Your aim?'

'To take the enemy's helm, sir,' said the First Lieutenant, 'assisted by Mr. Tomlinson here.'

Tomlinson was a friend of Tom Potts. They were both midshipmen, and shared a midshipman's berth aft. Corrie was coming to know everybody in the ship. She could not see the First Lieutenant nor Tomlinson clearly at this moment because both their faces had been smeared liberally with burnt cork, and all of the ship's lights and fires had been put out, plunging the vessel into darkness. She could just make out the white dress of the First Lieutenant's wife Anne who was watching the departure of the cutting out expedition from the forecastle, and seemed to be wearing the same dress as before, or one very like it, and on this occasion appeared to have left her hat in her cabin.

The White Lady is blessing our going forth. I hope her power is strong tonight. If only she could come with us.

'No more sounds of any kind,' said the captain. 'I don't want to hear that bell again. You there in the chains, whisper what you find.'

'Aye aye, sir,' said the leadsman.

'Jensen, your job?'

A large Danish sailor grinned. 'To cut the cable to her anchor,' he said, hefting his axe by way of demonstration.

'Everybody remember to yell when you board,' said the captain, finally, when he came to the end of the line.

'We'll scare them buggers to death,' said one of the sailors.

'Silence, Hargreaves!' growled Midshipman Potts. 'You heard the captain. No talking.'

MIDSHIPMAN HARRIMAN 95

Potts appeared nervous. If this was the young man's first cutting out expedition, Corrie could well understand his fear, for this was her first, too, and she felt a sudden urge to go the head, and had to strive to suppress the inclination.

I hope I don't disgrace myself during the fight.

The expedition took to the boats.

The ship's jollyboat and launch set off into black billows upon which danced the reflections of the bright stars of Orion's belt, flashing and flickering like mad, pulsing fireflies.

Looking up at the night sky, Corrie was dazzled by the sight of more than two thousand pinpricks of light shining down on her from the heavens. Only at sea and at war, when the lamps of your ship have been extinguished and you venture forth in a small boat before the moon rises, are you rewarded by a vision of a cosmos that stays with you for the rest of your life. Corrie thought of the stars as candles glowing in the windows of the city of God. She knew that Cassiopeia, the wife of Phoenix, was holding one of those flickering candles, while Virgo, Persephone's mother, was holding another.

I'm glad there are women up there, looking down on us from the gods. I hope I impress them tonight as I strut my piece upon the boards down here on Earth.

Corrie was puzzled by a great belt of misty light that stretched all the way across the sky from one horizon to the other. She had no idea what that belt might be, but had no time to ponder the matter further, for she had to row.

Her muffled oar, its pins wrapped in oakum to keep them from squealing, was a brute to handle, and she had to keep rigorous time with the rower seated on the thwart before her, and she had to remember to feather her oar at the right moment. If she made one mistake with her oar there might be splashes that would alert the enemy as to their coming, and prove fatal.

She had read in one of her father's books that surprise was half the battle when falling upon an enemy ship at night.

Corrie pulled on her oar.

I shall have to fight like a man. I wish I knew more about fighting. I wish I'd paid more attention to my fencing master, Mister MacGregor, back in St. John's. I do remember him telling me to keep my fencing arm bent slightly at the elbow.

She pulled on her oar again.

I'm in a strange situation. Captain Redburn is a handsome fellow but he thinks I'm a spy, my master-at-arms is a homicidal lunatic who has tried to drown me, my brother is a confused and angry young man whose brains have been addled by a blow to his head, and, as for me, I'm a crazy girl who has joined the navy to fight the French, a girl who hardly knows her own father.

She pulled on her oar once more.

Would she ever see her father again? Had he been hurt when the *Queen Charlotte* went up in flames? Where was he now? She had never seen much of her father, he being a serving naval officer, but had always felt confident that he would return one day and tell her the truth about her mother.

I'm on my way, Dad. I'll find you. You wait.

In, out. In, out. For a while, the rhythm of the rowing lulled her into a feeling of security, but then she began to hear the roar of breakers close at hand and to feel the loom of something ominous.

Somewhere in the black night a foreign voice spoke. '*Qu'est-ce que c'est?*'

The dark side of a ship towered before them. This must be the supply ship, thought Corrie. She could just make out the ship's name, GALATÉE, painted on her bow in white lettering with curlicues. She wondered what the name meant, if it meant anything. Not all names can be translated, she reminded herself. Sometimes they are just names.

'*Qui va là?*'

Corrie knew what *that* meant. She heard a note of alarm in the watchman's voice.

The strake of their launch scraped against the stern of the supply ship.

This is it. We're here. Now I must get the job done.

'*Merde!*' said another voice. She heard running footsteps crossing a deck and then the clamor of a ship's bell being beaten madly.

Ting-ting-ting-ting-ting-ting-ting!

Corrie saw Jim leap up from the boat and use that rickety cutlass given him by the master-at-arms to slash a hole in a boarding net rigged by the *Galatée*'s sailors to impede attackers. She saw her brother spring through the gap in the torn netting and land on his bare feet on the enemy's deck, yelling like the captain had told him to.

She wanted to follow her brother through the netting, and to watch his back for him, but she knew she had to scramble up into the enemy's shrouds instead, and this she did, her fingers and toes feeling for the ratlines in the dark.

Billy and the other topmen are close behind. I'm glad I'm the first. I'm glad I'm leading the way up into the yards. I hope I don't meet any Frenchmen.

Crack! Something slammed into the mast beside her head and she felt a burning pain in her left arm.

Ouch! That hurt! Somebody is firing at me.

A dangling bight of rope bumped her cheek.

Just as the captain predicted, the French have slackened off the footrope and left it hanging down in a lubberly loop. I must be halfway up to the yard by now.

Popping sounds broke out below, and there was much banging and clattering as if pots and pans were being thrown about in a galley brawl. Then there came a cry of anger, followed by a sudden crash of something heavy falling and breaking on the deck.

She got a whiff of gunpowder up her nose that made her think of Guy Fawkes, the revolutionary Catholic who had tried to blow up the House of Lords in the palace of Westminster.

Her heart hammered as she passed the foremast cap.

I'm scared.

Of course she was fearful. She was on a French ship, clambering about on alien spars at night. Was this her enemy's foretopsail yard before her, this strange dark pole shutting out the stars and cocked up at such an odd angle?

Of course it's the yard. What am I waiting for?

Her heart in her mouth, she ran to the end of the long timber. She went down on her knees and felt about in the dark with one hand.

I have to help unfurl the sail.

IX

HER frantic fingers found the furled sail, and then, heavens be praised, she came upon the cord securing the bunched up canvas to the yard. She loosed the knot that held the sail and felt some of the canvas fall away. She heard it flap once in the night wind, sending a shiver through the yard on which she was perched.

The sounds of the fighting on deck are growing louder. Jim is down there somewhere in the thick of that fight. I wish I could help him.

That wound to her brother's head might slow his reactions, rendering him unable to fend for himself.

Her fingers went exploring again. She discovered that the footrope was still made fast to the yard at this end, even though the sailors of the *Galatée* had slackened it off and had left the line hanging down from the yard in a big bight that reached nearly down to the deck. She began hauling in on that line, taking up some of the slack, a daring plan forming in her mind.

We're all here. I'm not alone. I can see Billy.

Her fellow topmen had followed Corrie's example and had dashed out onto the yard, and she could see them casting off the remaining gaskets. They let the canvas fall.

Shadowy figures on the yard below, figures with blackened faces, went to work to set the sail to catch the breeze.

The newly unfurled sail stiffened and took the strain.

Here we go!

Corrie felt the supply ship heel over. Where now was that big axe-wielding Danish quartermaster Mikkel Jensen when he was needed? Wasn't he supposed to be severing the anchor cable? Any more delay by the Dane and the *Galatée* would be taken aback and brought up all standing.

Chop that cable, Mikkel! I'm waiting.

Consumed with anxiety, Corrie looked down to see if she could spot the hulking Dane. She did not see him at once, but spied instead several members of the expedition fighting for their lives, their darkened faces grim in the light of a single lantern that swung from a stay. She saw a man run through, and heard that man's despairing cry. She jumped to her feet, the bight of the footrope in her hand. Was that Jim down there?

'Jim!' she shouted. 'Look out!'

She missed her footing, tripped, and fell across the yard. The impact forced the wind from her lungs, and she lay face down, draped across the spar, gasping and struggling for air.

I have to breathe! Jim is in trouble. I have to get back on my feet. I have to save my brother.

Above the din of battle Corrie heard a solemn thumping begin.

Thwock, thwock, thwock…

She risked another look down, and this time she saw the Dane. There he was, Mikkel Jensen. He was forward by the bitts, and he was striking at the hawser of the *Galatée* with his axe.

Good for you, Mikkel! Another few blows like that and she'll be ours.

Corrie licked some of the bitter burnt cork from her lips as she jumped back up onto her feet.

Mikkel Jensen swung his axe one more time: Thwock!

A sudden shock was transmitted through the timbers of the supply ship as the hawser parted.

The *Galatée* heeled over in earnest and began to sail.

Corrie staggered and nearly lost her footing. Staring downwards, she saw the door to the French captain's cabin swing open, flooding the deck with lamplight. A straight-backed figure leapt out onto the deck, his sword in his hand. This was the French captain. He was dressed in a coat with a high collar, broad lapels and a double row of buttons down the front. On his head he wore the kind of cross-wise hat Napoleon had worn while crossing the Alps into Italy. His brightly polished shoe buckles shone.

He's come on deck, with his men, to drive off the English marauders. He plans to take back his ship.

Corrie saw a brave English lad, his face smeared with black, block the French captain's way.

Corrie's heart gave a leap in her chest.

It's Jim. He'll be killed.

The French captain's sword flashed in the lamplight. Her brother tried to parry with the useless cutlass issued to him by Augustus Sly, the basket-shaped guard of Jim's weapon shattered at once and the cutlass fell to the deck in pieces. Her foolish brother did not flee. Instead, he stood his ground and balled his fists.

'You fool, Jim. Run away! The French captain will kill you. Jim!' cried Corrie.

Desperate to save her brother, she flung herself bodily from the yard. The air tore at her clothes and whistled in her ears as she plummeted towards the deck of the French ship. She was an avenging angel swooping down from the stars.

I'm an avenging idiot. I'm going to hit the deck and die a horrible death.

She held on grimly to the bight of the footrope.

Blocks squealed.

The footrope stripped skin from her palms.

I'm coming, Jim! I'm on my way!

She had only seconds in which to save her brother from the French captain.

She saw the French captain raise his sword to strike her brother down.

Am I in time?

Corrie swung across the crowded deck like a swinging pendulum, kicking out to right and left. She sent two sailors flying, and then, like a hawk falling upon some lesser bird, caught the French captain unawares, striking him in the chest with both feet.

Got you!

The force of the impact sent the poor man flying over the ship's rail. His sword flew from his hand and landed with a clatter on the deck.

The surprised French captain cried '*Au secours!*' as he went over the side, and Corrie heard a splash as his body hit the water.

She let go of the footrope and teetered on the ship's

rail, flailing her arms, trying to keep her balance.

I hope I am not going to join the French captain in the sea. Water is my enemy.

'Jim! Help me!'

Her brother sprang to her side, grabbed her arm, and yanked her down off the rail onto the deck. 'Corrie! Are you all right?' he asked, his black-smudged face inches from hers.

'Find the flag halyards,' she told him, wrenching her arm free of her brother's grasp and snatching up from the deck the French captain's gleaming, burnished sword. 'Remember your orders. The flag halyards will be near the quarterdeck, handy for the signalman. The *Galatée* is under way now but she's not ours until you bring her flag down. Hurry!'

Jim nodded.

He snatched a belaying pin from a nearby rack and ran aft into the thick of the fighting, brandishing the wooden pin as if it were a sword.

Corrie followed close on his heels, sword in hand.

A crowd of armed Frenchmen with pale faces charged down the deck towards them, shouting '*Galatée!*' A French lieutenant led the onslaught.

'*Swift!*' yelled Jim by way of reply, and laid about him with his belaying pin.

Billy Brown and a dozen other top men came swinging down from the rigging in the same reckless way that Corrie had, swinging across the deck and kicking out at white faces as they came. They helped themselves to bars of solid oak from the ship's capstan, and laid about them with a will.

'*Allez! Allez!*' shouted the French sailors, turning to counter this new threat.

Corrie slashed and thrust madly with her stolen sword. She was frantic with worry. She feared the crew of the *Galatée* might take back control of their vessel and bring to naught all of her efforts, and all of the efforts of her shipmates.

She and Jim managed to break through the press of men.

They burst onto the *Galatée*'s quarterdeck.

A French sailor smashed a bottle of red wine upon the ship's binnacle, and then lunged for Jim's head with the shattered remains of the bottle. Jim tried to ward off this savage attack with his wooden belaying pin, only to have the pin knocked from his hand.

Billy Brown came to Jim's rescue. She gave the French sailor a terrible blow that sent him flying.

'Was that the Dutty Duppy?' asked Jim, shaking his numbed hand to try to bring it back to life.

'That a bad boy, that Dutty,' said Billy Brown. 'Now you go change that bad boy's flag for him.'

Jim dived for the flag lockers.

Suddenly a pistol went off at close quarters.

Corrie spun on her heel. The French deck officer had fired at Tomlinson.

She saw the young midshipman fall.

Corrie was filled with rage.

You bastard.

She raised her stolen sword high and brought it down hard on the wrist of the Frenchman who had fired the shot. The man's eyes opened wide. He dropped his pistol and held onto his wounded wrist with his free hand. Lieutenant Keeper pushed past Corrie, grabbed the wounded French officer by the neck and dragged him bodily away from the *Galatée*'s wheel.

The guns of the fort lit up the night.

A rumbling thunder shook the air, and something struck the ship's spars a heavy blow.

'Sir!'

Corrie gave the Lieutenant a shove.

A falling spar came crashing down onto the quarterdeck in a tangle of splinters. The spar missed the Lieutenant by inches but a stray block slammed into the French helmsman and knocked the unfortunate man senseless.

'Thanks, Harriman,' said the Lieutenant. 'The wheel! Check the wheel!'

Corrie leapt over the fallen spar, ran to the ship's wheel and spun the spokes experimentally. 'Still responding, sir,' she reported.

'Good,' said the first lieutenant. 'Jensen, steer us out.'

'Aye aye,' said Jensen, and the big man laid his axe gently on the deck, took hold of the body of the downed steersman by his collar, dragged him out of the way, and took over the wheel from Corrie.

'South west by south,' said the Lieutenant.

Corrie nodded. Yes, that was the course she would have taken to rendezvous with the *Swift*. She watched the big Dane peer through the shattered binnacle glass at the trembling compass needle and at the card. Could he see which way the compass was pointing with so little light?

'South west by south it is, sir,' said Jensen.

Corrie looked about, surprised. A change had come over the vessel. All was quiet. The fighting was done. The guns of the fort had fallen silent. All Corrie could hear now was the rhythmic slap-slap-slap of the waves under the *Galatée*'s stem. She loved that sound. It meant that the ship was on the move.

What happened to Jim? I lost track of Jim.

She looked over her shoulder and there was her brother. He was standing by the jackstaff. Behind him, a white ensign, newly bent on, was fluttering bravely in the dawn breeze.

'God save the King!' her brother shouted. 'Hip-hip…'

'Hurray!' shouted the black-faced officers and men of the *Swift*'s cutting out expedition, and the cheer was repeated for a second and a third time.

'Well done, Jim!' said Corrie, absurdly pleased that her brother had not only kept his head but had very sensibly run up the English flag, and then taken it upon himself to call for resounding cheers in order to demonstrate to all of the sailors, both French and English, that the *Galatée* had been taken.

Some of the French sailors took one look at the British ensign bent on by Jim, scrambled up on the rail, and dived headlong into the sea to rejoin their captain, while others, unable to swim, and therefore unable to escape, stood in a dispirited group by the forward hatch.

Corrie could see the dismay written on their faces.

We have captured their ship. I'm not surprised they look so glum.

Corrie looked down and was surprised to find that she still held the French captain's sword in her hand.

What am I to do with it? I'm an ordinary seaman, not an officer. I don't need a gentleman's sword.

'Secure the prisoners!' ordered Lieutenant Keeper, and Corrie went to work with her shipmates to confine the remnants of the French crew below and to set a guard over them. All of the French seamen wore male attire, but Corrie noticed that one sailor in particular had a wet look in her eyes and a protruding stomach. Corrie gave her an encouraging smile, but the woman shook her head and made the sign of warding.

That is one brave lady.

Corrie remembered reading in a newspaper about a certain Mrs. Mackenzie, a brave Scottish woman who had given birth in the middle of the battle on the Glorious First of June. Mrs. Mackenzie had been delivered of a baby boy in the bread room of the *Tremendous*, and, to commemorate that auspicious birth, her child had been christened Daniel 'Tremendous' McKenzie. Young Daniel Tremendous Mackenzie would be six years old by now.

Corrie grinned to herself.

I bet the boy is still in the navy. Perhaps I'll meet him.

The prisoners having been made safe, and guards set over them, Corrie joined her brother on deck, where she laid the gleaming sword on the planking, having no scabbard to put the blade in, nor any sword belt to buckle it on with, for that matter.

She and Jim walked to the weather rail and watched dark green crabs scuttle about on floating islands of wrack, as the *Galatée* stood further out to sea, towing the jollyboat and the launch behind her.

Corrie and her brother looked at the crabs so they would not have to look at the remains of Tomlinson, lying there on the quarterdeck in a pool of blood, unseeing eyes staring at the breaking dawn.

'That was awful,' said Corrie.

'You shouldn't be here,' said Jim hotly. 'You shouldn't have to see these things. There are reasons the navy is forbidden to girls.'

'That master-at-arms issued you with a useless weapon,' said Corrie.

'What did you expect?' her brother asked.

'I don't know. Captain Cook discovered the Vegetable Sheep.'

'He was killed for his trouble.'

'I know. But when you read Mottley, it all sounds so important: fighting the libertarian French, saving the world from Bonaparte. Even the names of the ships are stirring: *Neptune*, *Revenge*, and the *Royal Sovereign*. I had no idea how violent a simple cutting out expedition can be, nor how desperately committed one's shipmates have to be in the heat of action. You know that Billy Brown risked everything to save us. I wonder what Lieutenant Keeper will tell the captain when he makes his report. I hope he gives Billy the credit she deserves.'

'He'll tell some cock and bull story,' said Jim. 'He

knows better than to report what really happened. Nobody ever does that.'

Corrie heard a sour note in her brother's voice that seemed to confirm her suspicion that Jim had been badly shaken when his feeble weapon had been broken and he had found himself battling the French captain of the supply ship with his bare hands. Probably he was bitter because a mere girl had come to his rescue, and his own sister to boot. That was not the way things were supposed to happen, not in a man's world. Poor Jim must feel like a fool, and he must fear to be taken for a fool by his captain.

I wonder what kind of report Lieutenant Keeper will make?

Both Corrie and Jim were within earshot half an hour later when Lieutenant Keeper spoke to Captain Redburn, and they both heard him describe in curt and unsentimental terms the taking of the French supply ship *Galatée*.

They heard the captain of the *Swift* acknowledge the report, and wondered if their captain would press for details about the *Galatée*, her tonnage and her cargo. It was not every day that a vessel fell into Redburn's hands that might bring him a pretty penny in the Admiralty Prize Court, a court that might award the captain up to two eighths of her assessed value. They were pleasantly surprised when the captain refrained from demanding those details, and showed himself more interested in people than in prize money.

'The Tomlinson boy was killed?' was the captain's first question.

'Pistol shot to the chest,' said Mr. Keeper. 'The purser is getting him ready for burial.

'I'm very sorry to hear that,' said the captain. 'Tomlinson was a promising lad with the makings of a fine officer. And Ebbs and Giovanni?'

'Not seriously wounded, sir.'

'You did well, Keeper. Let me have your report in writing by noon.'

'Yes, sir,' said the lieutenant. 'Thank you, sir.'

The captain ran his eye over the blackened faces of the members of the cutting out expedition. 'Well done, lads! Your expedition was a success and you have every reason to be proud. Hand in your weapons and wash your faces.' The captain turned away and spoke quietly to his first lieutenant. 'How did the Harrimans do?'

X

'BOTH Harrimans did well, sir,' Keeper answered. 'Jim Harriman saved me from a falling spar, and Corrie Harriman knocked the captain of the *Galatée* clean over the side and into the sea.'

'Bless my soul!' exclaimed Captain Redburn. 'Knocked their captain overboard, you say?'

'Yes, sir.'

'Well I never did!' he exclaimed, and walked over to the poop rail to examine the captured supply ship in the light of the dawn. He could see some damage aloft, and the footropes would have to be re-hung. 'A midshipman's command,' he decided, 'with a prize crew of ten. Do you think Potts could take her to Halifax?'

Prizes were routinely taken to the navy station in Halifax for adjudication, and for the incarceration of prisoners of war.

Potts, Corrie reminded herself, was that young fair-haired midshipman who had caught her eye. She strained to hear the lieutenant's reply.

'I think Potts could manage that, sir,' said Keeper. 'Do him good to have the responsibility. He spends too much of his time gadding about in the tops and telling jokes.'

'So I'd noticed,' said the captain dryly. 'Tell Potts to report to me in my cabin, and you send me Corrie Harriman, too. I'll see them both together, after they've cleaned up.'

'Aye aye, sir,' said Keeper.

Corrie and Jim looked at one another.

Corrie mind raced. She hardly dared to hope that her status in the *Swift* was about to change, but she could tell by Jim's expression that he thought that likely in view of the captain's order that she and Potts were to attend him *at the same time*. Instead of being happy and excited for her at this prospect, her brother was understandably upset.

She believed she knew what was going through his mind. Traditionally, the navy was forbidden to women. Men might con their ships, men might climb masts, men might lead boarding parties, men might fight sea monsters and come home ashore afterwards for tea, but women? Would you believe it? Women had to stay ashore to boil the kettle, women had to make the gravy, women had to sweep the hall, and that was not fair at all.

Jim had agreed with his sister on countless occasions that the way the navy treated women was unjust, but now, faced with the reality of sharing a navy career with his sister, and faced with the disconcerting prospect of her imminent promotion at his expense, he felt she had taken her revolutionary ideas too far.

From Jim's point of view, Corrie had overstepped the bounds of decency. She had saved his damned *life*, and that was not the way things were supposed to be. It was not natural. Damn it, but for her, he would be *dead* at the hands of that French captain of the *Galatée*. And why did that make him so upset? Here she was, his own sister, ruining *his* career in the navy.

That, Corrie believed, was how this turn of events

looked to her brother Jim. Her brother felt that the captain should be asking to see *him* in his cabin, not her, and found this trick of fate utterly infuriating. Jim was deeply disturbed that such a thing should be allowed to happen, for it upset his faith in men.

There was nothing Corrie could do for her brother, no way for her to make amends. She felt for him, she really did, and was painfully aware that she might be about to turn his world upside down.

'Jim, I'm sorry,' was all she said. What else could she say? In the garden of their father's house, under the pergola, looking out over the lake, they had taken turns reading the ballad of Sir Patrick Spens, the best sailor who had ever sailed, the brave Scottish gallant who had gone down with his ship. Her brother at this moment must be feeling like Sir Patrick Spens *when the lift grew dark, and the wind blew loud, and gurly grew the sea.*

'It may turn out all right in the end,' she said, although she did not really believe that. Sir Patrick Spens had been drowned.

'Just so as we understand one another,' her brother retorted, and she could hear the acrimony in his voice, 'I don't want any more of your *help*. Go and wash the cork off your face. The captain's waiting, and, if you don't hurry, that fellow Potts will arrive before you do.'

In this her brother was prescient. Scrubbing her face and washing the worst of the blood from her jacket took Corrie longer than she had expected, perhaps because she had been up all night fighting the French, and her left arm, grazed by a round, was stiff and sore.

She arrived at the door to the captain's cabin to find midshipman Potts waiting in his best uniform, with his buttons polished and his shirt freshly laundered.

'Sorry I kept you, Mr. Potts,' she said, a little out of breath, tugging her own clothes straight and nodding to the marine on guard.

It was not Sergeant Deering this time, she was thankful to see, but another, younger marine who rapped smartly and said 'Mr. Midshipman Potts and Ordinary Seaman Harriman.'

'Show them in,' she heard the captain answer, and the door was flung open and in they went.

'Sit on the lockers,' said the captain.

They sat on the lockers. The door closed behind them and they were alone with the captain in one of the few places in the *Swift* that afforded real privacy.

Corrie grinned to herself.

We must make an interesting contrast, Tom and I. Beside me, seated on the far end of this locker, is a happy-go-lucky curly-haired boy dressed in a well-tailored midshipman's uniform, his cocked hat under his arm, while here am I, seated at this end, an apprehensive ordinary seaman decked out in the purser's slops. I am sure that by now Potts has learned that I am woman pretending to be a man. I see it in his eye. If the captain was not sure if I was a woman before the taking of the Galatée, *I think he is sure of it now. Someone has told him. He is avoiding my eye. The master-at-arms has told him, or the White Lady. I wonder how Captain Redburn will treat me now, and why has he called me here together with Midshipman*

Potts?

'These are your written orders, Mr. Potts,' said the captain, handing the young man a sealed letter. 'You are required to take command of the prize and to sail her to Halifax, there to report to Admiral Collier. You may choose ten men for your crew. Mr. Weevil will help you choose.'

'Thank you, sir,' said Potts, taking the envelope and staring at it as if it were going to bite him.

Corrie had a fair idea of what the young man was thinking. His first command! What was he to do with the French prisoners? What if the wind changed? Whom should he choose to sail with him? Would the crew do what he said? Would they respect him?

Corrie sat very still, wondering what was going to happen next.

Am I to be sent with him? Is that why I'm here? What has the captain in mind? Is he about to ship me off to the admiral in Halifax so that the admiral may return me to St. John's on some passenger boat suitable for the fairer sex? That would give my brother a chance to make his own way in the navy!

The captain took a slip of parchment, wrote on it in ink, blew on the ink to dry it, and passed it to Potts. 'This is your course for Halifax. Keep a close watch on the prisoners. Give them half a chance and they'll put you over the side the same way we put their captain over the side. Speaking of which,' he said, turning to Corrie, 'how exactly did you manage to push a full-grown man, armed with a sword, into the sea?'

Corrie thought of her rash decision to leap from the

yard to save her brother, of the headlong plunge she had made down towards the *Galatée*'s deck with only the loop of slack footrope to slow her descent, and of her mad swing across the deck that had ended so unfortunately for the French captain.

'I don't know, sir,' she answered honestly. 'I think it was a stroke of luck. I hope the French captain could swim, sir. I could hear waves breaking. The shore must have been close.'

'A stroke of luck,' the captain repeated, and regarded her solemnly for a moment. 'Yes, I dare say it was a stroke of luck, and I wish all my crew were as lucky.'

Corrie gawked at the captain, waiting to see what he would say next.

I know what he can't say. He's thinking of Tomlinson. That boy did not deserve to die. He was young, and his end came so suddenly. 'Damn this war!' was what the captain wanted to say, but to voice such a thought might be construed as treason.

The captain continued to regard her thoughtfully. He was taking stock of her.

'Mr. Potts is about to depart for Halifax, so I'm going to need a midshipman to replace him. Could you fill his shoes, Harriman?'

Corrie leapt to her feet. Her head hit the deckhead.

'Owch!'

She had forgotten how little headroom there was in the captain's cabin.

She sat down again in a hurry, rubbing her head.

'You mean me?' she went on, hardly daring to believe she was hearing correctly. 'You're making me a midshipman?' She stared at Potts and then back at the captain. 'Yes, sir. I'll do my very best, sir. But...'

Words failed her.

'But what, Midshipman Harriman? What's the matter?'

'I don't have a uniform, sir.'

The captain raised an eyebrow at Midshipman Potts.

For a moment Potts looked lost. He was, Corrie supposed, busy trying to work out in his head how he was going to sail the *Galatée* with only ten men to work the ship *and* to guard the prisoners. Nobody would get any sleep at all, and if they ran into bad weather, his goose would be cooked. Potts's face cleared as he stemmed the tide of his thoughts, returned to the present moment and cottoned on to the captain's unspoken request.

'Oh,' he said. 'I have a spare uniform in my sea chest. You can borrow that if you like, Harriman.'

'Are you sure?' said Corrie, turning to Potts.

A ray of sunshine from the nearest stern window had turned Potts's hair gold again. He looked so dashing. Maybe it was those blue eyes of his.

You're charming in your boyish way, Potts.

'The coat collar is a bit worn,' said Potts.

'That won't matter,' she said, and she gave him a big smile.

'You're more than welcome,' said Potts, and smiled back at her in a way that made her quite sure he knew she was a girl.

Sizing him up, Corrie judged that he and she were of about the same size and build, so Potts's spare uniform might fit her well.

A uniform will make me look more like a man, and I'll be a junior officer. I'll be giving orders instead of taking them. But where shall I sleep? Not in the manger, surely.

'You'll have the Midshipman's Berth to yourself, ' said the captain pointedly, as if he had read her mind.

Startled, Corrie gave the captain a sharp look. Of course, she reasoned, the *Swift* was a small ship, with room to berth only one or two midshipmen. Was that why the captain was promoting her, to give her a chance for privacy? Having her own cabin might prove of advantage in playing the part of a man, but she disliked the thought of being promoted just because she was a woman. She hoped she was being promoted for her actions during the cutting out expedition. She decided to give her captain the benefit of the doubt and to acknowledge his consideration *and* his kindness.

'I hadn't thought of that,' she said frankly. 'I am doubly grateful, sir.'

'Don't thank me,' said the captain darkly, holding up his hand as if to ward off her appreciation. 'It is not going to be a bed of roses, as Mr. Potts will surely tell you. You'll have to stand watch, Mr. Harriman. I won't tolerate any lazy midshipmen in my ship. There will be arduous lessons for you in mathematics, seamanship and navigation. Did they teach you navigation at your spy school?'

'Sir?' For a moment, Corrie was taken aback.
He's joking. I'm a fool.
'I can take a running fix, sir,' she said, 'and I know about leading marks and lines. But I'd like to learn about strategy. May I borrow a book about that, sir?' she asked, glancing avidly at the books in the captain's becket.

I want to read all those books, every last one of them.

The captain took a slim leather-bound volume from his collection and handed the book to her. 'I lend you this for your edification. Pay particular attention to the pages dealing with the arc of fire, and return the book to me when you have read it. I shall question you on the contents.'

'*An Essay on Naval Tactics by John Clerk of Elgin*,' read Corrie, tracing the gilt lettering on the spine with her forefinger. 'I haven't read this one. It was not in my father's library. Thank you, sir. I'll look after it, I promise.'

'You had better,' said the captain. 'Now off you go, both of you, and report to Lieutenant Keeper.'

'Aye aye, sir,' said Midshipman Potts, clutching his orders and his slip of parchment tightly in one hand and his hat in the other. Terror warred with ecstasy on his face. The young man was about to command his own *ship*.

'Aye aye, sir,' said Corrie, clutching the captain's book as greedily as Potts was clutching his orders, and wondering most earnestly if the boy would have time to lend her his uniform *before* he had to go into the

Galatée as her commander. She simply *had* to have a proper uniform if she was to play the part of an officer.

Jim is going to kill me.

She kept her head down as she left the cabin. The captain had solved two problems at once: what to do with his prize, and what to do with the girl sailor. Now he would be unrolling some chart or other, perhaps a chart of the entire Gulf of Saint Lawrence, and bending over it to figure out what he might do to thwart the plans of his enemy, Frigate Captain Jean-Pierre Troude, whose ship carried a greater weight in metal than the *Swift* did, and more sailors.

War with Revolutionary France had taken on new urgency since Napoleon Bonaparte had seized power in November. Corrie did not know the wording of Admiral Collier's orders, but could guess from the action in which she had just participated that those orders had to do with intercepting supplies destined for the French islands of Saint-Pierre and Miquelon, the only territories not ceded to the British in the Treaty of Paris, and just about all that remained of New France.

Captain Redburn must have every reason to suspect that both food and ammunition would be on their way to the islands, sent in secret by those eager to restore French power. The supplies would be crammed into the holds of coasters of shallow draught like the *Galatée* that would hug the shore by day and seek the protection of shore batteries by night.

Not far from their present position lay the fort and dockyard that had once been the heart of French power in this region, and might be so again.

Captain Redburn might be setting to work with dividers and rule to plot a course to the Bay of Plaisance. That is where Corrie would take the *Swift* were she in his shoes. That was where the French would be waiting, she felt sure.

As she followed Potts down to the midshipman's berth, they passed the captain's steward, Harbottle, bearing the captain's breakfast on a tray, and Corrie was surprised when Harbottle stepped aside to let them pass. She really had been promoted.

I'm an officer now. People make way for me.

XI

CORRIE wondered if the steward Harbottle would disturb the captain and break his train of thought when he delivered that breakfast? She hoped he would not. A clever servant would tell the marine not to knock, enter the cabin unannounced, as servants were allowed and encouraged to do, and lay the captain's breakfast tray quietly on the upholstered seat under the great stern windows, and then leave without the captain, bent over his chart, ever having noticed his servant's coming or his going. After that Harbottle would, she had no doubt, return to the galley and report to the cook: 'Captain's up to summat. He's got his charts out. Them Frenchies had better watch out' or words to that effect, whereupon the cook would add some fresh charcoal to the fire in the ship's cooking range and say 'Hear about the new middie?' Gossip spreads fast in a warship.

Still keeping her neck bent and her head down, Corrie followed Potts into a tiny cabin. The boy fumbled with a hanging lantern and soon a soft amber glow filled the small space.

Corrie explored the little cabin with her eyes.

This is my cabin now. That bunk looks tempting. I've been up all night. But I must stay awake. I have to have a proper uniform to wear if I'm to be an officer.

There was only one place to sleep in the cabin, she saw. Potts and Tomlinson must have shared that single mattress, taking turns to sleep on it, watch and watch about. Their two sea chests stood side by side in a corner, forming a makeshift seat. In another corner, mounted on a metal ring firmly fastened to the bulkhead was a wash basin in which there stood a white pearlware jug decorated with blue figures depicting a parson, a clerk and a sexton. Near the brass-handled door, a carved giltwood mirror hung from a peg on the bulkhead. The mirror swung lazily this way and that with the motion of the vessel.

Corrie placed the book the captain had lent her on top of the hand-woven linen pillowcase at the head end of the bunk, and gave the pillow a squeeze. It felt quite soft, and was stuffed with goose down, to judge by a few feathers that escaped and floated for a moment in the air before drifting down to settle on the deck.

She watched Potts drag his dark green painted pine sea chest out into the middle of the cabin by one of its two rope side handles. He turned the key in the lock. He flung open the flat hinged lid.

'These might fit you,' he said, and laid out on the bunk the clothes and appurtenances of an apprentice officer: a pair of pinchbeck shoes, a puritan high felt hat that tapered towards the brim, a long-tailed blue uniform coat, a white shirt with pointed collar, a close-fitting white waistcoat (*I wonder if I'll fit into that*) with double rows of shiny buttons, white pantaloons, buttoned at the knee, a black stock and a pair of silk stockings.

'I'll try to repay you at the first opportunity,' she said. Such an outfit must cost a small fortune.

'There'll be no need for that,' said Potts off-handedly. 'These togs are getting old anyway, as you can see. Not much left of the cuffs. Pater will buy me some more if only I can bring the *Galatée* safely into Halifax.'

'Give Cape Breton a wide berth, watch out for the sand banks, and you should do fine. Who are you going to choose for your crew?'

'I'd better leave that to the Weevil, I think' said Potts, closing his chest and locking it. 'Good luck, Harriman.' He shook her by the hand, stepped out of the cabin and collared a passing sailor to carry his chest up to the waist. He was taking the rest of his belongings with him on the prize.

Once the sailor had left with the chest, and Potts had dashed up the steps to begin his new duties, Corrie closed and locked the door and stood for a moment alone in the cabin, her arms crossed and her hands on her shoulders, staring down at the clothes Potts had laid out for her on the bunk.

She was terrified.

This is how an actress like Hannah Pritchard must feel in her dressing room, making ready to get into character and to take to the boards. How do actresses do that? How do they pretend to be other people? I don't know. I'm not sure if I'm ready to be an officer, but there's a war on, and sometimes you have to do things in war that you would not even think about doing in times of peace.

Summoning up her courage, Corrie took a deep breath, made sure the door was locked, and then took off the seaman's jacket, breeches and the hat she had chosen from the slops in the laundry, and began putting on Potts's clothes. She pulled on his silk stockings first, and then his pantaloons. The pantaloons fitted well enough, and the buttons were easy to fasten. Next she wrapped his black stock three times around her neck and tucked it up under her chin.

Then she pulled on Potts's shirt and adjusted the frayed cuffs. The shirt was the right size, but the collar took a few minutes to adjust. She had to make sure the high points looked smart without stabbing her chin. Grimly she buttoned up his waistcoat tightly, squashing herself to do so.

Ouch! Lucky I'm not as big a woman as Norah.

Next she pulled on the heavy blue uniform coat with its twelve big wide shiny brass buttons, a coat that she trusted would serve her well in all weathers.

She went to the mirror and liked what she saw. She looked like a young man, except for her straying hair. She had to do something about that. She took up Potts's high felt hat, settled it firmly about her ears, adjusted the curled brim, and then tucked the loose hairs away under the hat. That was better. Now she really could pass for a man. There was nothing to be done about the bone structure of her face, but there were men who had rounded cheeks and full lips. She would have to pretend she was one of them.

Somebody knocked on her door. She took one last look in the mirror to be sure of herself, and reached for the door handle, her heart beating rapidly.

My life as an officer begins. Who knocks on my door? Will they see through my disguise?

She opened the door.

It was her brother. He had brought her the French

captain's sword, complete with a scabbard and a belt. His eyes widened when he saw her. A look of concern crossed his face. Confronted by her uniformed figure, he had thought for a moment that he had made a mistake and had knocked on the wrong door.

'Sorry, sir,' he began, and then his jaw dropped. 'It's you,' he said, astonished. 'It really is you. I didn't know you. You look...amazing.'

'Of course I do,' she whispered. 'Come inside and close that door. Turn the key in the lock.'

Jim did as he was told.

Corrie could tell by the expression on her brother's face that he could hardly believe what he was seeing. This was his own sister, but she looked just like a man, a real midshipman. She had the white patches on her collar, and the fashionable felt hat, and everything was, well, perfect, except that she lacked a gentleman's sword, and Jim had brought that sword with him: the sword of the French captain of the *Galatée*. The weapon would add a convincing touch to her costume.

Jim handed her the sword. 'Sly tried to grab this, but I told him an officer wanted it. The scabbard and belt I found in the arms chest. You really do look the part. When you opened the door, I thought...'

'What did you think?'

'I thought you must be an officer I hadn't met yet, I really did.' He paused, uncertain of how to go on. 'I thought you were a young man,' he said lamely.

'Good. I'm glad I fooled you. I hope I can make others think of me in the same way. Just about everyone in the ship knows who and what I really am, thanks to Norah in the laundry, but if I look the part perhaps I can earn their respect.'

'Wherever did you get the uniform?' asked Jim, his eyes darting to the remaining sea chest standing by the bulkhead at the far end of the cabin. The chest had H. TOMLINSON painted carefully on its lid.

Corrie followed his glance. 'I never thought of that,' she said and shivered. 'Potts was kind enough to lend me his gear. I've promised to repay him when I can. I'll have to do something about the cuffs, though.'

Jim looked his sister in the eye. 'I'm glad it was Potts who came to your rescue, and you didn't have to dress up in Tomlinson's clothes. That jacket fits you well. You might have had it tailor-made. Bless my soul. My sister is a midshipman and I'm...' He paused. 'I'm an ordinary seaman.'

'You're jealous,' she said.

'It doesn't seem fair.'

'I know. It should have been you. The way you stood up to that French captain.'

'It isn't that. The French captain would have killed me if you hadn't come flying down out of the rigging and knocked him overboard.'

'I hope the Frenchman reached the shore,' said Corrie. 'I hope I did not cost him his life.'

'Me, too,' said Jim, a little surprised to find that he agreed with her. One was supposed to hate one's enemy, but that did not seem right, somehow.

Corrie slid the sword into its scabbard and belted it on around her waist. 'Thanks for this handsome weapon. I shall need it for formal occasions, and, more important, I shall need it when we go into action again, and when we do, we must make sure you have a decent weapon to fight with, too. No more falling-apart cutlasses. Don't be angry with me, Jim, if I have to give you orders.'

'I'll obey them.'

'Sit down,' said Corrie. She seated herself on the bunk and indicating the sea chest with a wave of her hand.

Jim sat on the sea chest.

Brother and sister faced one another in the tiny cabin. Here was a chance to chat, if they spoke quietly so as not to be overheard. As they sat, their bodies moved to counter the unceasing rhythmic movements of the ship. They did not have to think about this. Their bodies behaved automatically. Corrie and Jim had become used to the continual swaying of the *Swift*.

There was a moment of silence as they looked into one another's eyes. They had not been alone together since Lieutenant Keeper and his press gang had burst into the Crown and Anchor.

'It all started in the pub,' said Corrie.

Jim nodded. He knew their adventure had begun in the tavern but could not remember clearly what had happened.

Corrie told him.

The sailors had rushed into the inn. They had brought with them the smell of tar and brine, tobacco and rum. Their faces had been wet with rain. They had held belaying pins tightly in their fists.

What a life-changing moment that had been! One

glance had told Corrie why Lieutenant Keeper had brought his party to the Crown and Anchor. The whole story had been written on Keeper's face. His captain had sent him to find sailors, and by God he was going to find sailors! Corrie had not found it in her heart to blame him. Navy ships were often hard pressed to find enough crew to make up their complement. She had guessed then and there that this press gang was from the frigate that had sailed through the Narrows into the port of St. John's two days earlier, and had been busy taking on water and provisions.

'Run!' Corrie had whispered in her brother's ear.

'We can fight them,' Jim had replied angrily, and had balled his fists, that brave fool of a brother of hers.

'Don't you remember what happened to Farrel and Power?' Corrie had reminded him.

Jim's eyes had widened at that. Six years earlier Garret Farrel and Richard Power had been hanged and dissected by surgeons for murdering a lieutenant named Lawry who had been in charge of a press gang one evening, and had returned next day to help a newly impressed sailor pack his belongings. Jim recalled the awful occasion all too clearly. It had been the talk of the town.

'The kitchen,' she had said, on that night of their impressment. She had grabbed her brother and they had dashed through the swing door into the pantry. They had darted by the Bodley range, sending one of the brass cooking pots flying.

'Mrs. Anderson!' Corrie had shouted.

The proprietor's wife, Bessie Anderson, had been

busy taking some flipper pies out of her oven. The aromas had tickled their noses: hot flaky pastry and smoky meat. The room had been full of steam and there had been wonderful bubblings. Bessie was a great cook.

'You're not going home the once?' Bessie had said, waving away the steam with her hand and looking up at them in a bewildered fashion. 'You won't be staying for a feed of my sea parrot and lamb's tails?'

'The press gang's come, Bessie,' Corrie had blurted out. 'Can we get out by the back door?'

Bessie had nodded. 'It's not locked,' she had said. 'That was a grand dance, the pair of youse,' she had shouted after them. 'A fine hornpipe and a natty bit of work on them costumes by your Mrs. Demeter. You look just like two sailors.'

'Thanks, Bessie,' Corrie had shouted back, and had reached for the door handle.

The back door of the pub had burst open in her face, and there had been Sly, the ship's master-at-arms, and his accomplice, the big burly sailor named Foster. The pair had been sent around to the back of the building to catch any runaways.

She had disliked Sly from the moment she had set eyes on him. She had wanted to wipe the gloating look off the man's face. Her brother, always the rash one, had thrown himself forward and butted the master-at-arms in the stomach, hoping to create enough of a diversion to let his sister get away.

But the master-at-arms had been too quick. He had seized Corrie's arm with one hand and grabbed Jim by the hair with his other hand.

'Give this boy a taste of your billy, Foster,' he had said, and he had smiled a cruel smile.

'No!' Corrie had cried, struggling to go to Jim's aid.

Then Corrie had seen the club come down on her brother's skull with a sickening thud and had felt the pain of the blow as if she herself had been struck. 'You didn't have to do that,' she had said to Sly, shaking with anger.

'Friend of yours?' the master-at-arms had asked, licking his lips.

'My brother,' Corrie had answered, blinking back tears.

'Two for one, then,' the master-at-arms had replied smugly.

The press gang had shepherded the newly pressed men down to the stone quay and into the launch. One of the seamen had carried Jim over his shoulder because Jim had been unconscious. They had been rowed out to the *Swift* by the light of that great bronze moon.

'So that was how it was,' said Jim.

Corrie nodded.

She wondered if Sly had guessed then that she was a girl and had decided to go ahead and have her carried off to the ship anyway? In retrospect, she was glad Sly had made that decision, but she had serious doubts about his motives. Had Sly planned from the start to humiliate her and to take advantage of her? That shifty look in his eye had to have meant something. Perhaps throwing her into the bilge hole had been the beginning of a bizarre courtship. She felt a shiver go down her spine.

Now that I am properly disguised, and wearing this uniform of an officer, and have my own cabin, I trust Sly will leave me alone. If he does approach me again, then Jim and I may have more trouble on our hands.

'We'll have to deal with Sly,' she said, voicing her thoughts.

'Yes,' her brother replied. 'Sly is dangerous. He won't hesitate to tell the Admiralty who you really are, and when the navy hears that you're a woman they may stop your pay. Only men are allowed to draw pay, and, as a midshipman in a sixth-rate, if I remember correctly, you'll be earning one pound, fifteen shillings and sixpence a month, starting from today.'

'How do you like my new quarters?'

Jim took a good long look around the cabin. 'Cramped,' he said. 'But at least they have given you somewhere to sleep. They haven't allotted me a hammock yet, and after that fight for the *Galatée*, I'm dead on my feet. I dare say it's back to the manger for me tonight, to bed down in the straw with Campbell and the other animals.'

'You could share this cabin with me,' said Corrie.

Jim grinned. 'Share a berth with an officer? Are you out of your mind? The captain would have me shot.'

Corrie sighed. 'It's...' She paused, searching for the right word. 'It's so *wrong*, being thrown into the navy like this. Mrs. Demeter must be worried sick about us. Bessie Anderson at the inn will have told her about the press gang. Mrs. Demeter may be writing to

Mum and Dad right now.'

There was a moment of silence while Corrie and Jim imagined their governess seated in the summerhouse, dipping her pen in an inkwell and frowning as she composed a letter telling their parents what had befallen them. What were the odds of such a letter being delivered? They could not be high. The whereabouts of their parents were uncertain, and the *Queen Charlotte* had blown up. Their governess's letter might take months and months to reach Mum and Dad, if it ever reached them at all. Mail was chancy in wartime.

'We're on our own until her letter reaches them,' said Jim, mirroring her thoughts. He leaned against the bulkhead and closed his eyes. He began to snore.

Corrie sat down on her bunk bed, taking care not to crease the tails of Potts's coat. She tucked the goose down pillow behind her head, and found it most comfortable.

She, too, shut her eyes and began at once to dream. She was in the orlop of the *Swift*. Between two kegs she came across a heap of ash shaped like a volcano. Creatures crawled out the top of the mound of ash. She tried to catch the creatures and put them back where they belonged but the creatures would not go back inside the ash heap. The ash heap began to smoke. The ship was on fire! She ran to a ladder and began to climb for help. The ladder grew longer and longer as she climbed. Somebody started shaking the base of the ladder. The ladder rattled. A voice said 'I know you're in there.'

She woke up, gasping. Her uniform felt strange and heavy on her shoulders. She was sweating.

'Jim!' she said, jumping to her feet. She shook her brother's shoulder. 'Wake up! Somebody is trying to break into the cabin.'

XII

A SLURRED voice said 'I know you're in there.'

The handle of the locked door turned, and Corrie and Jim, startled from their nap, watched the handle move. The door shook. Someone was indeed trying to break in. But who?

'Who's there?' said Corrie loudly.

'Open the door, Miss Harriman. Open up or I'll have you in the brig.'

'It's Sly,' whispered Jim. 'He's been drinking. I heard Mr. Weevil recommend Sly's crony Foster for the prize crew for the *Galatée*, so Sly is probably on his own.'

'Time we turned the tables on this so-called master-at-arms,' said Corrie, making up her mind. She was now a midshipman, a King's officer. No longer did she have to put up with the likes of Sly. It was time to brave it out and teach the man manners. 'Unlock the door, Jim,' she said quietly, straightening her uniform and filling her lungs.

Jim raised his eyebrows. 'Are you sure?' he whispered. 'I'm not supposed to be here, remember? I'm just an ordinary seaman.'

'You're not just an ordinary anything, Jim. You are a seaman under my orders. Unlock the door.' She pulled Potts's hat down firmly about her ears, tucked in her stray hairs, and turned to face the door.

Jim turned the key. The door flew open.

Corrie confronted the master-at-arms.

He is alone. His eyes are bloodshot. A vein is

throbbing at his temple. His breath smells of rum. I'll face him down, the bastard.

Sly leaned heavily against the door, and tried to focus. The figure before him was not what he had expected to see.

'Blimey, what's this?' he said, staring at her. It was the first time he, or anybody else save for her brother, had seen Corrie dressed in uniform.

Sly pushed himself away from the jamb and made an effort to stand upright and to straighten his shoulders.

He shook his finger at her waggishly. 'Oh, no, my dear,' he went on. 'Don't think I don't know what you're up to, dressing up in Tom Potts's old clothes. You can't fool me. You can't fool old Sly. Oh, no! You're no officer. I knows all about you. Put you in the bilge hole I did, with the rats.' Sly laughed and then grabbed at the doorjamb to steady himself as the *Swift* shouldered a wave. 'You and me's going to have a private word or two in this cozy little cabin of yours. We're going to be real snug, you and me.' He put his finger to his lips. 'Mum's the word, eh?' he said, and suddenly lurched forward into the cabin, his face taking on a look of cunning and avarice.

'You are a disgrace to your profession, Mr. Sly,' said Corrie sternly. 'You have been drinking. Leave this deck at once. Obey me or there will be profound consequences. I warn you in all seriousness, Mr. Sly, that I consider you unfit for the post of master-at-arms. I shall be reporting your misconduct to the First Lieutenant. Now do as I say and leave! That's an order.'

'Leave?' said Sly, and rolled his eyes. 'Oh, I fully intend to leave, my pretty, just as soon as you and me have had our little *parlez-vous* together. We is going to be as snug as a bug in a rug, we are. Just the two of us.' With these words the boozy master-at-arms had the audacity to grab Corrie by her shoulders. 'Wot you got under this fancy rig, eh?' he said, pushing her back deeper into the cabin.

Jim, who had been hidden behind his sister, stepped into view. 'You heard what the lieutenant said, Sly. Get out!'

'You young whelp,' said Sly, puzzled, and doing his best to focus on Jim. 'Where did you come from? Oh, I see. In the cabin with her were you, eh? Oh, dear. Did I interrupt something?'

Jim saw red.

'Don't,' said Corrie, putting a warning hand on Jim's arm.

But Jim was too enraged to heed her. His anger boiled over, just as it had done in the Crown and Anchor on the night he had been taken by the press gang. Inflamed by rage he could not contain, furious at the insult to his sister, Jim punched Sly hard, right on the jaw. He put all of his pent-up fury into the blow, striking out at this damned fool of a master-at-arms who was threatening his sister, and quite forgot in the heat of his anger that striking a warrant officer was a crime punishable by death.

The blow sent the boozy master-at-arms flying backward and Corrie heard a hollow *thwock* as Sly's skull hit the carriage of a carronade.

'You've killed him,' whispered Corrie, and she covered her face with her hands. Peering between her fingers she could just make out the prone form of the master-at-arms lying there stretched out on the deck. The man did not move. He just lay there. She hoped Sly was dead, for if the master-at-arms regained his senses and managed to recall being hit by Jim, Corrie was sure there would be hell to pay. Jim would be brought before the captain.

She removed her hands from her face and glanced up and down the deck. Nobody was about. That was lucky.

I'm an officer. I have to do something. I have to take charge and give orders. That is what officers do in a crisis, and this is a crisis.

'See if he's alive,' she said.

Jim knelt by the prone form of the master-at-arms and placed a hand on the man's neck. 'I can feel a pulse.'

'More's the pity. Jim, do exactly as I say. Run to Billy Brown. Tell her that Midshipman Harriman wants a word with the Captain of the Maintop right away. Tell her where to find me, and ask her to bring two, strong, trustworthy hands along with her when she comes. Hurry, but don't draw attention to yourself. Go!'

Jim leapt to his feet. 'Billy Brown, and two trustworthy hands,' he said, repeating her order in the tradition of the navy, and left at the double.

Corrie found herself alone with the crumpled form of Augustus Sly.

I should kill the brute before he wakes. Jim could die for this. But I can't bring myself to do further harm to this unarmed man lying helpless here on the deck, no matter how much I loathe Sly, and I do loathe him. I despise him most deeply.

The man was an oaf who deserved to die, but she could not bring herself to kill him, not while he lay helpless like this. Sly was her shipmate, when all was said and done, and this was her first day as a midshipman.

I have to behave like an officer, but not a ruthless officer. Hurry up, Billy. I need you. I need another woman. We have to solve this problem before the men do something really stupid like hang my brother for defending his own sister.

She stood there waiting for what seemed an age, and then she heard a patter of bare feet and sighed with relief. Here came Billy Brown striding down the deck towards her, with two of her largest top men, barrel-chested William Ferris and broad-shouldered Jas Ludford.

Corrie knew both men to be reliable, discrete hands. They would have to be, to cope with a situation like this.

Billy Brown took one look at Sly lying there and turned to Ludford. 'Got your tot?'

Ludford fished about in a pocket of his sea trousers and produced a hip flask in which he had hoarded his daily ration of spirits and water, meted out to him by the purser from the rum tub at noon.

'Pour your grog over this man's chest,' said Billy

Brown. 'I'll give you my ration tomorrow.'

'You can have my tot, too,' said Jim.

Jas Ludford grinned and upended his flask, sousing Sly's shirt and jacket. 'He's had a hard night, has old Sly,' he said, and laughed.

'Ferris. Ludford. Carry the master-at-arms to his cabin,' said Billy Brown, 'and stow him in his bunk.' Billy Brown turned to Jim.

Jim stood there rubbing his sore hand. Hitting Sly had hurt.

'Thank you Billy,' he said, shame-faced.

'No bother,' said Billy Brown. 'If this bad boy wake up with one big headache, we tell him the Dutty Duppy Man did it.'

Corrie laughed. 'I hope he believes you, Billy,' she said. 'I've had all I can take of Mr. Sly.'

Billy Brown snorted. 'If that Sly make more trouble, then we make more trouble for him. Now you come with me, Jim. I show you how we splice the mainbrace.'

When her brother and the others had left, taking the unconscious body of the master-at-arms with them, Corrie sat on the edge of her bunk and put her head in her hands.

Sly knows I'm a girl. My uniform didn't fool him. Sly would never dare lay his hands on Anne Keeper, who wears a gown embroidered with designs depicting palmetto leaves, Grecian vases and lyres, and has a shawl draped around her shoulders and a lace bonnet with a pretty bow tied under her chin. The very trappings that make Anne the White Lady keep men like

Sly at bay and serve to remind them of the dire consequences of having their way.

The penalty for attacking a lady was as severe as that for stealing a sheep; and a man caught doing either might expect to be hanged. So why did Sly think that she, Corrie, was fair game?

Because I am dressed like a man, that's why. I should have hit Sly myself. I should not have let Jim risk his life. Next time, if there is a next time, I'll be the one to punch Sly in the face. I'll be the one to put him in his place. Warrant or no warrant, I'll lay that foul master-at-arms out on the deck and teach that tipsy oaf a lesson.

She paced, head bent, up and down the confined space of the midshipman's berth, her hands behind her back, thinking hard. Next time she confronted Sly in front of other people, she would have to make him sorry for his impudence. She would have to teach him to respect women, and by God she would do that, and when she had finished with him, there would be no more sneers from Sly, no more calling her 'miss' and no more of his smarmy advances. She was a midshipman, now, and she must act like one.

When tiredness overcame her, she stopped her pacing, took off her coat, hung it carefully from a peg, and lay down on her bunk. She put her head on the soft pillow and dreamed that she was back in the *Galatée*, but this time she had taken Potts's place, and was on her way to Halifax. Sly was at the wheel, and asking her what course he should steer. She reached into the pocket of her uniform jacket for the scrap of parchment the captain had given her with the course written on it, but her pocket was empty. She did not know what course to steer! She tried to remember the chart, but all the numbers on the chart were crawling about like a disturbed ant's nest. In desperation she looked up at the stars for help but the stars were laughing at her. She felt a hand on her shoulder.

'Anne?' she said sleepily. 'Anne Keeper?'

She woke from her dream, sweating and frightened.

It is morning. I have to pull myself together. I am an officer. Sly tried to attack me. Jim hit him. I hope Sly is dead, for if he is not, I fear there may be hell to pay.

She put her coat on and left her cabin, more angry with herself than with her brother or that miserable master-at-arms. She encountered scores of seamen going about their business, and, yes, they stood aside to let her pass. From the break of the poop she watched men pour up from the lower decks carrying their hammocks to the bulwarks to provide breastworks while leaving the gun decks clear in case of a call to action.

The Scottish sailor Campbell doffed his bonnet and said to her: 'Message from the captain. He wants you to report to him in his cabin, sir.'

'Thank you, Campbell,' said Corrie, and she headed aft for the captain's cabin.

Now I am to face the music.

Every morning Captain Redburn and his first lieutenant Keeper dealt summarily with the ship's miscreants in the relative privacy of the captain's cabin.

All those who had committed any one of a host of minor sins of omission and commission to be expected in a ship of one hundred and eighty-four men, women and children, had to have their cases heard and appropriate punishments meted out. On some days there were three or four offenders, according to Billy Brown, but today there might be but one, and that one would be her brother. Corrie had no doubt that she had been summoned to act as a witness at Jim's trial.

I have to save my brother's life. I have to say the right thing.

The marine at the door let her in without question. What a difference a uniform makes! The captain's cabin was much as she had last seen it. The bed was still a mess, and the charts were still strewn upon the window seat. Looking down at one chart, she saw that the numerals representing the soundings were staying perfectly still and behaving themselves. She was not dreaming.

I'm awake. This is real. Jim is on trial for his life. He's standing respectfully in the middle of the cabin with his hat in his hands.

'I'm surprised to see you here, Harriman,' said the captain, frowning at Corrie's brother, who had a glassy look on his face. 'What's all this about, Master-at-Arms?' the captain inquired, turning to Sly, whose head had been spectacularly bandaged. 'Why are you laying charges against this man, and of what is he accused?'

'At seven bells in the last dog watch,' said Augustus Sly, 'while going about my duties, I was struck without provocation by this here ordinary seaman Harriman and I fell down and hit me head, sir. When I came to, the boy was gone.'

Sly is lying. He must have woken up in his cot, stinking of rum. But will the captain believe Sly? Sly is the ship's policeman. The captain is bound to take his word for it. I am filled with fearful apprehension.

Captain Redburn turned to Jim. 'This is most serious, Harriman. Striking a warrant officer is a capital offence. I can have you hanged. What have you to say?'

Jim stared at the captain. His mouth opened and shut but no words came out.

'The lad is tongue-tied,' said the captain and turned to his first lieutenant. 'What has the Lower Deck to say about this?'

Lieutenant Keeper replied: 'Drunk and disorderly. Outside the midshipman's birth. Witnessed by the midshipman, sir.'

'I see. Well, Midshipman Harriman, perhaps you can enlighten us as to what happened? Your brother here is accused of striking the master-at-arms.'

'He came to my rescue, sir,' said Corrie, her cheeks burning.

The captain's eyebrows shot up. 'Were you in danger?'

'I was at risk, yes, sir. The master-at-arms was trying to break into my cabin, sir.'

'Whatever for?' said the captain.

'He was shouting. He was incoherent. He smelled of drink, sir.'

'Were you in your cabin at the time?'

'I was, sir. When I heard the master-at-arms

shouting I unlocked my door and told him he had been drinking and ordered him to leave.'

'Was your order obeyed?' asked the captain.

'No, sir, it was not. Instead of doing what he was told, the master-at-arms seized me by my shoulders. It was then that my brother intervened.'

'What have you to say to that, Master-at-Arms?' asked the captain, turning to the bandaged policeman.

'Pack of lies,' snarled Sly. 'Never been anywhere near her.'

'Near *him*, you mean,' said the captain.

'If you say so, sir,' answered Sly cheekily. 'Never been anywhere near *him*.'

The captain swung round to take another look at Corrie. He paused to take in her seemly appearance, her smart clothes. Yes, Potts's old uniform seemed to fit her well enough, he must be thinking. She looked like an officer. She looked like a man. By her blazing cheeks he knew her to be furious and yet she was acting and speaking in a levelheaded fashion She was definitely officer material. He had not made a mistake in promoting her.

Corrie returned her captain's frank look, raised her chin and waited. She knew the captain was making up his mind as to what had really happened the night before, and that he must be wondering whom to believe and whom to blame. How he judged her character, and the character of her brother, would be important in deciding the matter.

'Can anyone confirm what you say?' the captain asked her carefully.

'You might want to ask Billy Brown, sir,' she said.

'Billy Brown?' said the captain, surprised. 'The Captain of the Maintop?'

'Yes, sir.'

'The midshipman's berth seems to have been a lively place last night. Pass the word for Billy Brown.'

'BILLY BROWN!' shouted the marine sentry. 'PASS THE WORD FOR BILLY BROWN!'

The call was taken up by other members of the crew, and soon the Captain of the Maintop joined them the cabin. The captain could hardly fail to notice that Billy Brown had appeared with an alacrity that suggested she had been waiting close at hand and had been expecting the summons.

The captain explained to Billy Brown the nature of the charge against her maintop man and asked if she had visited the midshipman's berth at the time of the incident.

Corrie could hardly breathe.

It all depends on Billy now. I hope she says the right thing.

XIII

'YES, captain,' said Billy Brown, hat in hand. 'I visit the midshipman's berth.'

'What did you see?'

'I see that bald-head master-at-arms, Mr. Sly,' she said, waving her hat at the gentleman in question.

'And what was the master-at-arms doing when you saw him?'

'That man he bleach hard last night. That man he stretched out on the deck outside the midshipman's door, sir. He do nothing.'

'Lying on the deck doing nothing, you say. Why?'

'Wanty, wanty, can't get it, getty getty, no want it.'

'Explain.'

'That facety bald head he fell down and knocked himself out. I smell the rum on his breath.'

'The boy hit me!' shouted the master-at-arms, and pointed an accusing finger at Jim. 'I wants that lad flogged.'

'Billy, did you see this man Harriman strike Mr. Sly?'

'No, captain.'

'Mr. Sly, did you try to enter Midshipman Harriman's cabin?'

'I can go anywhere I like. I'm the master-at-arms.'

'Answer my question, Mr. Sly. Did you try to break into the officer's cabin.'

'I had to make an arrest.'

'Was Jim Harriman in the midshipman's cabin?'

'They were in there together, getting up to

mischief. I had to do something about it.'

'What kind of mischief?'

'All kinds, sir. Them two have been nothing but trouble since they joined, sir. Cheeky brats. I don't know who they think they are.' He grabbed a handful of Jim's jacket.

This time Jim was able to control his anger. Corrie could see that he wanted to fight back but made an effort not to do so. Jim must know as well as she that the master-at-arms was trying to provoke him into doing something for which the captain would *have* to punish him.

So instead of resisting Sly, her brother pursed his lips at looked levelly at the captain over Sly's shoulder in the hope that the captain would grasp what was really going on.

Corrie was terrified. Her brother's life hung in the balance. Her brother did not deserve to be punished, but the navy was a hard and exacting service, and the authority of the ship's master-at-arms had to be upheld, no matter what. What was the captain going to do?

'Let that man alone, Sly,' said Captain Redburn, frowning at his belligerent master-at-arms. 'I should be more concerned about your own conduct if I were you. You tried to force your way into the cabin of Midshipman Harriman, and now you are trying to blame the midshipman's brother for an altercation for which you were entirely responsible. The task of a master-at-arms is to keep order among the ship's company. He is not supposed to create disorder. If the task of master-at-arms is beyond you, then I shall have to find someone else to perform your duties.'

'You can't do that,' said Sly, taken aback. He let go of Jim's jacket and swung around to confront the captain. 'Got me a warrant, I have.'

The captain raised his hands, palms upward, as if imploring the heavens to give him patience, and turned to his first officer. 'This won't do,' he said. 'This won't do at all. We need a new master-at-arms.'

'Mikkel Jensen,' suggested Lieutenant Keeper.

'That big Dane we recaptured from the French? The fellow who turned up among the prisoners of the *Albanaise*?'

'That's the chap, sir. He's a solid, dependable type. His English is good, he's built like an ox, and he's popular with the men.'

'Send for him now. I want this over and done with.'

'MICHAEL JOHNSON!' shouted the marine at the door, and Corrie heard the summons being passed from deck to deck.

The hulking Dane entered the cabin bareheaded. A slight smile played about the corners of his mouth as he took in the tableau before the captain: the irate Sly, the anxious sailor, Jim Harriman, waiting to hear his fate, and the two dutiful witnesses, Billy Brown and Corrie Harriman. Jensen had little difficulty in guessing what was going on.

'Jensen,' said the captain. 'I want you to be our new Master-at-Arms.'

'Aye aye, sir,' said the Dane respectfully. There was nothing else he could say. He had been given an order, and the captain's word was law. He might not want to be the ship's policeman, but there could be no questioning of the captain's decision to make him one. He had been a skipper himself in his boat the *Bardo*, and knew the importance of respecting the chain of command.

Corrie looked the Dane over. She liked what she saw.

I bet Jensen will make a good master-at-arms. He has an air of common sense about him.

'Your first task in your new post, Mr. Jensen,' the captain went on, 'is to arrest Mr. Sly. He is accused of assaulting a midshipman. He is to be confined until we reach a port where he can be brought to trial. I imagine you will find the key to the brig somewhere on his person.'

'Aye aye,' said Mikkel Jensen again, and grasped Sly's arm firmly with one huge hand.

'Hey!' said Sly, his face white with shock, trying to shake his arm loose and failing. Jensen had strong hands. 'Leggo. Wot you think you're doing? I'm a warranted officer, I am.'

'Warrants can be revoked,' said the captain, and hooked his thumb at the marine on duty outside his cabin.

The marine entered the room and came to attention. 'Sir!'

'We have a new Master-at-Arms. Assist Mr. Jensen with his prisoner.'

Sly was led away, protesting.

The door closed behind him, cutting off a string of

filthy oaths.

'Well, Ordinary Seaman Jim Harriman, you have been accused of disorderly conduct. What have you to say for yourself?'

'My fault entirely, sir. I am very sorry, sir.'

Corrie wanted to say something but she held her tongue. Only the captain could decide what was to happen to Jim.

'Yes, I rather think it *was* your fault,' agreed the captain, looking long and hard at Jim. 'You must learn to control that temper of yours. One more incident of this kind, and I guarantee your career in the navy will be a short one. Do I make myself clear?'

'Yes, sir. Perfectly, sir.'

'I don't want to see you on report again, Harriman.'

'Yes, sir. I mean no, sir.'

Corrie felt a glimmer of hope for her brother.

I think Jim is going to be let off. The captain must have been looking for an excuse to demote Sly for months, and this incident has provided the justification.

The captain and the first lieutenant stepped over to the stern windows for a private word together.

Through the glass Corrie observed storm petrels fighting for scraps in the ship's wake. Spray was flung up into the sunshine and made rainbows. Clouds were visible on the horizon. Possibly the *Swift* was in for a blow. Corrie closed her eyes to shut out the immensity of all that awful water, even as she strained to hear what the captain and the first officer were saying.

'I hope I've done the right thing,' she heard the

captain say quietly.

'Sly is plausible,' Keeper murmured in reply. 'He's sure to make trouble when we return to St. John's. I don't think we are supposed to put warrant officers in the brig.'

'Sly I can deal with. I was thinking of the boy.'

Keeper stroked his chin. 'He's a plucky lad, Jim Harriman. He stood up to that French captain on the *Galatée*. I'll keep an eye on him, if you like. He might make quite a useful able seaman or petty officer one day.'

'Watch him. Did you notice how much Harriman, our new midshipman, kept to herself? She's a strategist. She was careful not to say that her brother hit Sly. I'd have been hard put to save the boy if she had.'

'She might go far in the navy, if this war does not put an end to her,' said Keeper. 'She's ready to stand watch, in my opinion.'

'Try her tonight,' said the captain, and then, looking over his shoulder, he raised his voice and said 'You're all dismissed.'

'Aye aye, sir,' chorused Billy Brown, Jim and Corrie as they left the captain's cabin.

Corrie lingered just long enough to glance again at the chart on the captain's table. She saw that it was a careful copy of a survey put together by Captain Cook's team twenty-five years earlier. A ruled line indicated that the *Swift* was eastbound for the Bay of Plaisance, just as Corrie had foreseen. The *Swift* would soon be shaving Cape St. Laurence. Captain Redburn was on his way to see if the French had recaptured their old bastion, Fort Royal. A note scribbled in the margin said something about Troude.

Frigate Captain Jean-Pierre Troude was someone Corrie might expect to meet one day now that she was, astonishingly, a *bona fide* midshipman in the *Swift*. She had to wonder what sort of a man Troude was.

She left the captain's cabin feeling elated.

I'm going to stand watch for the first time tonight. I heard the captain say so.

Back in her cabin, she hung up her uniform coat again and sat on the dead boy's sea chest. She knew that the important thing before going on watch at night was to be well rested beforehand. She wasn't sure if she could sleep again so soon, but she would have to try. Naval officers had to be able to snatch sleep whenever they had the chance. Perhaps she could read herself to sleep? She opened the book on naval strategy that she had borrowed from the captain, adjusted the wick on the lantern and began study an account of Admiral Rodney's encounter with the French fleet off Martinico in the West Indies. '*At forty-five minutes after six in the morning,*' the admiral wrote, '*I gave notice, by public signal, that my intention was to attack the enemy's rear with my whole force.*'

A page later, the Admiral, still bearing down on the French ships, ordered his captains to steer for their opposite numbers, and at that point Corrie found herself disappointed in the admiral. She had hoped the admiral would break through the enemy line first. That was what she would have done, had she been there.

The reading was making her drowsy, just as she

had hoped. She lay down. Her eyelids grew heavy.

A turtle came into her cabin and started looking for his belongings. He talked to her in Greek about his wife. Corrie felt guilty about eating animals. Then the turtle gave her a stern look and said she should not push French captains into the sea. Finally, the turtle handed her a letter from Mrs. Demeter.

Corrie could not quite make out what the letter was about, for it was written in a language made of pictures. There were pictures of rays, of an eye, and of people with funny heads. She tried to decipher the message.

Mrs. Demeter was trying to warn her about something. Just when she thought she was on the verge of discovery, a monstrous wave carried Corrie overboard. She found herself struggling under the water. She could not breathe. Rats nibbled at her legs. Then she heard a strange thumping. Thump! Thump! Thump!

Someone was knocking at her door. The book had fallen from her hands. The lantern had burned out. She had slept all through the day and through much of the night.

She jumped to her feet and staggered. The ship had become lively during her long sleep. She flung open the door.

If that Sly has come to bother me again…

It was not Sly at her door this time, but Anne Keeper's small son, the lad who had fetched Billy Brown down from the maintop to demand her services from the Master.

'Hello,' she said. 'What's your name?'

'Fraser,' said the boy, his eyes like saucers. 'You look just like a man,' he said. 'Where did you get that uniform?'

She smiled at him. 'Do you have a message for me, Fraser?'

The boy screwed up his eyes and recited from memory: 'Mr. Keeper presents his compliments and says he wants to see you on the quarterdeck right away.'

'Thanks for the message,' she said. 'What time is it?'

'Eight bells in the Middle Watch,' said Fraser. He knew his bells. He could count up to twenty.

'Run and tell him I'm coming.'

Corrie pulled on her jacket and fastened the buttons. It might be cold and wet on a wild night like this. She wished she had gloves. She grabbed her hat and took the precaution of pinning the hat in place lest it should be blown off by the wind.

For the first time in my life, I'm going to be officer of the watch.

If it was four o'clock in the morning here in the *Swift*, and, back at home in St. John's, at this time of the night Mrs. Demeter would still be asleep, but Cook would be up stoking the range and kneading the dough for the day's loaves.

Corrie left her cabin and made her way forward to the quarterdeck. She had to stop and grab at a shot locker to keep her balance when the deck fell away suddenly. The seas had got up. She would have to be careful.

Young Fraser had darted ahead of her, pretending to be a pilot vessel guiding a big ship into a harbor, and looked back with undisguised impatience at his tow. *He had no trouble keeping his footing.*

The wind tugged sharply at her hat as she came out on deck, but the pin held.

Am I to stand my first watch now, in the dark like this, with a gale blowing? Well, why not? I've been out in worse weather on my uncle's schooner.

She staggered onto the quarterdeck and saw a dark figure waiting for her there. It was the first lieutenant. She saluted and said 'Midshipman Harriman, sir, reporting as ordered.'

'Thank you, Mr. Harriman,' said Lieutenant Keeper, his voice formal and exact. 'Eight bells and all's well. We are twenty miles south of the Chapeau Rouge. Our course is north east by east. We are bound for Plaisance and Fort Royal. If you need me, I'll be in my cabin.'

'Yes, sir,' said Corrie, very conscious of her borrowed officer's hat and coat, and feeling a perfect fraud. 'Sleep well, sir,' she added, thinking that might be a polite thing to say to someone leaving the deck after a long stint on duty.

'I shall try,' said the first lieutenant, and with that wry comment he vanished down the companionway steps, leaving the *Swift* entirely in Corrie's hands.

She blew on her fingers to warm them. The wind was bitterly cold. A slight dimming of the stars, a few of which were visible here and there through rents in the cloud, hinted at the coming of the day, but dawn must be hours away. She shivered.

I'm the watch officer. My childhood fantasies have come true. Here I am conning a real ship instead of an apple tree. How long will it be before we near the far side of the bay?

She pictured the captain's chart in her mind's eye. The *Swift* was sailing into the Bay of Plaisance. To the west must lie Cape Saint Laurence, quite close at hand, while to the east, far off to starboard, somewhere out there in the night, must be the towering cliffs of Cape St. Mary, teeming with nesting gannets. She was headed for what had been for years the most powerful French stronghold in all of Newfoundland, and might soon be again, if Troude's people had overrun Fort Royal as well as the Pointe aux Canons Battery on the island of Saint Pierre.

The news of a recent and devastating attack made by a French squadron commanded by a Vice-Admiral Joseph de Richery had stunned everybody in St. John's, that city she knew so well, that city that was largely administered by the Royal Navy and governed by the commander-in-chief of the station. The English had been driven out of the islands by Joseph de Richery, and now it seemed likely from the scribbles on Captain Redburn's chart that a Frigate Captain by the name of Jean-Pierre Troude was hoping to follow up Richery's bold attack by re-establishing a French presence in the region. No wonder, then, that the *Swift* was on her way to Fort Royal to determine whether or not that fort was in French hands. It was good thing Troude had no idea who was the *Swift*'s officer of the watch!

I'm lucky I know the name of the man at the wheel.

The man at the wheel was the new master-at-arms, Mikkel Jensen. She could discern Jensen's features by the lantern light. She watched him discreetly out of the corner of her eye as he glanced from time to time at the compass card. His huge hands spun the spokes gently to meet a wave and then again to ease the vessel down into the following trough. She noted how firmly he stood with his feet braced, alert for any warning sounds from aloft. She saw that Jensen was keeping the *Swift* near the wind but not too near, and thought she could trust him not to luff.

'You are a confident steersman,' she said at last, feeling the need for someone to talk to.

'I was master of my *Bardo* with a crew of my own, until a French Frigate Captain named Jean-Pierre Troude came alongside in his warship the *Tonnerre* and, boom-boom, he sink us, and then, boom-boom, he sink other boats he say are English. I tell him I am Dane, I tell him I am neutral, I tell him I am protected by law of sea but that no-good Troude he just shout "*Tirez! Tirez!*" and down she went, my poor *Bardo*. She was a handy smack.'

'It must be awful to lose one's ship,' said Corrie. 'What happened to you after that?'

Mikkel Jensen went on to tell Corrie how, after the loss of his *Bardo*, he had been made a prisoner of the French, only to be rescued by an English warship, the *Queen Charlotte*. Aboard the Queen Charlotte, he had volunteered to join the English navy, but had then been captured by the *Albanaise* during a ship-to-ship engagement, and then, a month later, to his great amazement, recaptured by Captain Redburn and the crew of the *Swift*. Jensen's tale was a long one, and helped to pass the night, and, when his tale was over, Corrie felt obliged to tell Jensen a few tales of her own.

She told Mikkel Jensen how her father, too, had served on the *Queen Charlotte*, and was able to say, thanks to Captain Redburn, that she had reason to believe that her father had survived the fire that had destroyed the *Queen Charlotte* last March. She kept to herself her secret fear that her father had been badly burned in that fire.

As they exchanged yarns, Corrie and Jensen became aware that the sky had turned pink in the east. They began to hear a great muttering of birds, and then, more alarming, the roar of breaking waves somewhere close at hand.

Corrie became worried.

I'm the officer of the watch. It's up to me. I have to do something.

XIV

'WE must be closing on the eastern shore of the Bay of Plaisance,' she said. 'I want a man in the chains.'

'John Eaves is a handy man with a lead,' said Mikkel Jensen.

'The Yeoman of Sheets?'

'He swing that lead real good, find bottom for you.'

Corrie turned to young Fraser, who was testing the hourglass. She waited until the boy had finished turning the glass, and made sure he had chalked the time correctly on his slate, before she said to him: 'Go and fetch John Eaves for me, Fraser. Tell him to tallow his lead. Run!'

Young Fraser repeated the order and ran below to rouse the sleeping sailor.

The sound of the breaking surf grew louder, and the strange muttering of the seabirds became a clamor.

'What birds are we hearing?' asked Corrie.

'Aalge we call them in my country,' Mikkel Jensen replied. 'Aalge birds, they nest on cliff ledges. I climb cliffs, steal eggs. Different colors. Loud birds. Make big noise at dawn.'

As if on cue, the sun rose, ringed in pearly mist, and in the faint first light Corrie began to see the seabirds. They were flying to and fro from twisted and dangerous pillars of rock that were veiled in spray. The rising roar of the surf and the growing outcry of the birds grated on her nerves. She felt on edge, poised. She was officer of the watch and she was conning the

Swift into the very heart of New France.

I must be ready for anything. We are at war. The French must be close by. Captain Redburn has brought us here to Plaisance to fight the French. I must not let my captain down. We are awfully near the shore, and the wind is bouncing back off the cliffs, but I want to edge a little closer...

'A quarter less seven!' sang out Eaves from down in the chains. 'Soft shell and stones!' and the man coiled his line and made ready to cast again.

Soft shell and stones? Our Swift *must be well nigh on the beach. I must take some of the way off her.*

Corrie made a speaking trumpet of her hands and spoke to the maintop. 'Clew up the course, Billy!'

'Aye aye,' came Billy Brown's voice from the maintop.

That meant hard work for her brother Jim and for the other maintop men up there, the dour Campbell among them, but it was work that had to be done, in Corrie's opinion, for she wished to expose less canvas to these fitful gusts and make the *Swift* easier for Mikkel Jensen to handle.

Far above Corrie's head, the topmen ran out onto the yards and went to work on the clewlines and buntlines. Hauling on the buntlines drew up the central part of the sail and spilled some of the wind.

Soon Corrie could feel the difference. The *Swift* lost speed and slid on through the mist under topsails alone, slipping through the water like a silent ghost. This was just what Corrie wanted.

The surf became deafening, and the birds raucous.

Corrie turned to the helmsman. 'How does she feel, Jensen?'

'Better, sir,' said the Dane, trying the wheel.

'Nigh on six,' sang out Eaves. 'Round stones.'

The sea bottom was shoaling fast.

Corrie became excited.

I'm taking a big risk. But if the French are here, then I intend to surprise them. This is my first watch. I don't want to send for the captain unless I have to. I can manage this. I must remember to breathe.

'Sir!' said Jensen, with a meaningful glance forward.

Corrie looked ahead and saw the loom of something solid in the sea smoke. 'Fraser,' she said. 'The telescope. Quickly.'

The boy passed her the spyglass and she put it to her eye. Her uncle had taught her the trick of keeping both eyes open when using the glass. She adjusted the focal length until the inverted image became sharper and easier to make out. If only somebody would invent a telescope that did not turn everything upside-down.

'I see three coasters, anchored in the bay. The mist makes it hard to see what flags they are flying. Wait. They are French. Beat to quarters!'

The Marine drummer, a boy of about nine, his hair still tousled with sleep, ran out on deck, came to attention, and began beating his tambour.

'Fraser, run to the captain's cabin. Tell the marine on duty you have a message for the captain. Give the captain my compliments. Say we have three enemy vessels in sight.'

'Your compliments, and three enemy vessels,' said the Keeper boy, and dashed for the companionway.

'All hands!' Her order was passed on by word of mouth from deck to deck.

'Clear for action!'

Seamen tumbled from their hammocks. Mess tables and chairs were folded away. Bulkheads were knocked down. The fires from the galley were dumped over the side, their cinders hissing as they hit the sea. The lids of the gun ports were raised and the guns were run out. The decks shook under running feet. Boys and girls strewed sand from pails upon the deck to give the gun crews a good grip. In the after cockpit the loblolly men pushed four sea chests together to make an operating table, and the cook arranged her knives and saws, ready to treat anyone who might be wounded. The crew of the *Swift* had no surgeon, their ship's doctor having been lost overboard off the Virgin Rocks, and no medical man having been sent by the Admiralty to replace him since, and no sawbones to spare in St. John's.

Captain Redburn ran up the steps and onto his quarterdeck, smartly dressed if unshaven, and took in the situation at a glance. 'Let me have that glass, if you please, Mr. Harriman,' he said.

Corrie handed over the telescope. 'The coasters are weighing anchor, but we are blocking their only exit from this bay,' she told the captain, 'unless they want to try to sail out through that narrow gap between the island and the shore. I wouldn't want to, sir.'

'Well done, Harriman,' said the captain. 'Well

done indeed. You must have shaved that point closely and come in quietly to catch them unawares like this.'

'The mist helped, sir, and so did the noise of the birds when the sun came up. Their cries masked the sounds of our approach.'

'Did they indeed? And how do you find watch-keeping, Mr. Harriman?'

'Exciting, sir.'

The captain laughed. 'Ah, Mr. Keeper. I'm glad you've joined us. How shall we deal with these three coasters Mr. Harriman has trapped for us here in the bay? They seem to be making for the beach. I suspect their crews have no desire to be our prisoners.'

'I don't blame them, sir,' said the first lieutenant with feeling, for he had been a prisoner himself.

A dull, flat report sounded over the water.

'They have fired a gun to alert the fort. What does that tell us, Mr. Harriman?'

'Fort Royal must be close by and in enemy hands, sir. If the mist burns off with the rising sun, we may find ourselves trapped here in the bay and under the guns of the fort. I should have thought of that. I'm sorry.'

'That's all right, Mr. Harriman. Don't take yourself to task. Look! They plan to smash the three coasters to pieces on the shore. If the French have the fort, then they will also have that village hiding behind those dunes. We shall soon have Irregulars to deal with. We may not have time to retrieve the three coasters, but I believe we can burn them. Muster the boats' crews. I'll take the pinnace. Lieutenant Keeper will take the launch. You'll command the jolly, Mr. Harriman. See that every man in your boat has combustibles: a flint, a striker, some slow match, and an axe. Place a keg of powder on the bottom boards of your boat.'

'Aye aye, sir,' said Corrie, and ran to obey. At the captain's order, the *Swift* came up into the wind and began to back and fill, holding her position not far from the shore in the growing brightness of the new day. The mist continued to give the scene a soft glow.

As Corrie paraded the crew of the jolly boat, and saw that one of the six rowers was her brother, she distributed the combustibles, explaining to each man what they were for. As she worked, she heard the patient leadsman Eaves, still down in the chains, sing out 'Five fathom. Sand.' Eaves would go on casting the lead until somebody remembered to relieve him of his duty. She was glad he was calling out the depth of water under their keel, for the *Swift* was hove-to close to the shore, and would be drifting slowly with the tide.

'Keep your combustibles dry, men,' she said, as she and her small crew jumped down into the smallest of the *Swift*'s three boats and took their seats on the thwarts. The barrel of powder was swayed down and placed on end in the stern.

'Ready all! Row!'

She put the tiller over and steered the jolly boat towards the nearest of the three enemy coasters. It was grim to see the vessel they were pursuing smash into the beach. Her mast cracked off with the shock of the impact, and her spars came tumbling down in ruin. The dreadful crash and the evident destruction of the little vessel made a heart-breaking sight, but Corrie set her jaw. Her captain had sent her to set fire to this vessel, and that's what she'd do. The fallen spars would fuel the fire.

The French crew of the wrecked coaster leapt ashore and ran in among the sand dunes, abandoning their broken craft. They vanished from sight, and Corrie hoped that was the last she would see of them. She had enough on her mind, trying to puzzle out what orders to give her crew of six when their jolly boat reached the beach.

How does one destroy a beached coaster? She had no idea. She had to render it useless to the enemy, she knew that. But how?

I'm the officer. I'm in charge. I'm supposed to know what to do with this keg of gunpowder between my knees. If I make a mistake, we'll all be dead. Maybe Jim can think of a way to blow up a stranded vessel. I hope so. I haven't a clue.

As soon as the keel scraped on the pebbles, she gave Jim a nod and he jumped into the shallow water and began to haul the boat bows first up onto the beach. His fellow seamen stowed their oars and jumped out to help him.

Corrie was last out of the boat, clutching the keg of explosive tightly to her chest. She had no wish to drop the keg, dangerous in itself and liable to explode if mishandled. It was a shock to feel solid ground beneath her feet.

I've grown so used to the swaying of the deck, this beach seems to me to be rising and falling with the movement of the sea. I suppose some part of me expects these rounded stones under my feet to behave like the deck, and that's why I stagger like a drunken sailor. Whatever I do, I must not drop this keg of gunpowder, for if I stumble and fall, I shall kill my brother, my crew and myself.

'Hargreaves and Campbell. Stay with the boat. Be ready. We may need to push off in a hurry. The rest of you, come with me.'

She lurched her way up the stony shore that had not long since been a part of New France and was now New France once again. She assumed that Troude had put a French contingent ashore and seized Castle Hill and Fort Royal. Now Troude would be relying on coasters like these three she had just surprised to provide food and other necessities to his new garrison. He was going to be disappointed.

She cast her eye along the shore and saw that both the other coasters had now been driven hard upon the shore and abandoned by their crews, their masts shattered and their rigging tumbled in disarray. She could see the first lieutenant and the captain leading their seamen up the rocky shore to set the ruined coasters ablaze, just as she was leading her own people up the beach to do likewise.

Corrie staggered and nearly fell. She heard a shout.

Somebody is calling out commands in French. I hear a trumpeter sounding the charge. I must hurry.

She ran to the stricken coaster, a stout brigantine, painted green. The name on her counter was *Le Navigateur*. The sorry vessel lay tipped over on her port side, her spars cracked off.

'Gillman, Forester, put your axes to work. Make a hole in her side to let a draught in. Jim, you're with me.' Still carrying the keg, she led the way along the sloping deck and down into the fumes and murk of the brigantine's hold. She stumbled over an amphora that had cracked and was leaking oil intended for hundreds of soldiers' stoves and lanterns. Bobbing about in the spilled oil were cups, plates, boxes of bonbons, and, of all things, a bird made of brass. Jim turned a key and the brass bird sang. It was a mechanical wonder.

'We don't have time for that, Jim. The French Irregulars are coming. What do we do with this?' She lowered the keg of gunpowder carefully to the slanted deck. The barrel sat there, ominous and deadly.

Thwack! Thwack! Gillman and Forester swung their axes. They shattered a strake and daylight streamed in.

'I don't know how to use the fuse. Let's just make a bonfire,' replied her brother, and he laid about him with his own axe, smashing to splinters an exquisite chair, upholstered in needlepoint, from the court of Louis XVI.

In frantic haste Corrie tore open a mattress and dragged out the straw, teasing it apart. She borrowed Jim's axe and stove in a container of Dutch *brandewijn*. 'That should make a hot blaze,' she said, and added to the heap an exquisite portrait in oils of a lady holding a fan, posed upon a hillside balcony somewhere in the Côte d'Azur. Her scarlet dress clashed with the aquamarine sea, and Corrie wondered who she was.

Was she Jean-Pierre Troude's wife, or his mistress? Something in her head said:

She is the Lady in Red. Behind every man lies the invisible power of a woman.

Jim knelt down, unrolled his bundle of combustibles, struck sparks from the flintlock, and blew softly upon a heap of glowing shavings until a curl of blue smoke arose.

Corrie watched with bated breath.

We could die right now. This is the dangerous part. I wish I wasn't here.

Jim placed the burning shavings carefully among the dry straw. The straw caught at once and flames began to consume the painted canvas of the Lady in Red.

Corrie caught her breath.

Shall I ever meet her in the flesh, this Lady in Red? She looks formidable. I feel her power. Her face is turning brown. She is bursting into flames. I have to get Jim out of here before this wreck blows up in our faces.

'Come on, Jim!' she said, grasping him by the hand and hauling him back up onto the crooked deck. The angry shouting of the Frenchmen sounded nearer now. 'Let's go!'

I must hurry. I have to get my men back to the jolly boat. That gunpowder must be feeling the heat.

She jumped down from the deck of the doomed brigantine and landed on the pebbled shore. 'Forester, that'll do. Gillman, back to the boat! Bring your axes, both of you. Run!'

They ran.

XV

BEHIND them, the brandy went up with a whoosh, and smoke began to pour in a thick, oily black cloud from the gaping hull of *Le Navigateur*.

They tore towards the waiting boat. Corrie was pleased to see that Hargreaves and Campbell had unshipped the rudder from its gudgeons and set the boat's stern to the shore, and were standing by, one to port and the other to starboard, to shove off.

'Good work!' she said, jumping into the boat over the transom, with Jim at her heels, and Gillam and Forester not far behind.

A cry of fury came from the dunes. Angry campaigners for the revival of New France charged down the dune, discharging muskets as they ran, and a musket ball thudded into the gunwale an inch from Campbell's knee.

'If the navy doesn't put us to death, these rowdy Frenchmen will,' said Campbell, prizing the hot ball from the wood with a pocketknife, and dropping it in his shirt pocket for a souvenir.

'Your oar, Campbell, and be quick about it. Give way, all!'

At Corrie's order, Jim and his five fellow oarsmen pulled with a will. The jolly boat shot from the shore into the breakers.

Corrie slid the rudder pintles back into their gudgeons and grabbed for the tiller, ducking down as she did so in the hope of confusing the aim of the Frenchmen. They were not, so far as she could tell, uniformed and disciplined regular troops of the French army, but merely local French-speaking farmers and fishermen who wanted Plaisance to remain in French hands so that they might trade once more with their country of origin. The captain had called them 'Irregulars.'

The Irregulars ran splashing into the breakers, firing and re-loading their weapons as they ran, but they were too hurried and too inexperienced to hit their marks, and far too late to grab the boat, thankfully.

Corrie steered for the *Swift*. She could see the ship clearly now. How beautiful she looked with the sun on her canvas, backing and filling to hold her position out in the bay. The mist had burned away entirely, as Corrie had feared it might, and now the gunners in Fort Royal held a coign of vantage. Was the ship within range of their big guns? Corrie was not sure. She put her tongue in her cheek.

I should not have brought the ship in so close. This is all my fault. I'm a fool.

She glanced over her shoulder. The French Irregulars were standing waist deep in the water, shaking their fists, waving their muskets and regaling the perfidious English who had set fire to their supply ships and were now rowing away unpunished.

Corrie was glad to see that all three of the *Swift*'s boats had cleared the shore, and all three were being rowed as fast as possible away from the smoking ruins of the beached coasters. She had a sinking feeling that they had a long way to row before they would be out of harm's way, and the spreading flames might reach that gunpowder at any moment.

Corrie gripped the tiller tightly, hoping for the best.
I wish I hadn't burned the Lady in Red.

'Row for your lives!' she cried urgently, and she slapped her palm upon the stern to give them the time. Her rowers redoubled their efforts. Sweat poured from Jim's brow.

A colossal hammer blow struck the jolly boat, throwing the rowers into confusion and flattening the sea for a mile in every direction. Corrie's ears sang with a bang almost too loud for human ears to bear. Broken timbers and other remnants shot up five hundred feet into the air in a great cloud of smoke and then came raining down. Something very heavy landed with a crash on the foreshore, killing several of the Irregulars. Something even heavier smashed into the launch, narrowly missing Lieutenant Keeper but striking dead the man seated next to him in the stern, his long-time assistant, the ship's second lieutenant, Robert Forbes.

Corrie barely had time to think about this serious loss to the ship before two more colossal explosions shook air and land, and yet more debris fell around her, splashing into water. Then the bay went mad, breaking into waves that chased one another this way and that, and smashed into one another at random.

This is what it must have been like when the fire reached the magazine of the Queen Charlotte. *Poor Daddy! I feel like I want to throw up. But I can't. I have my duty to do. I have to see this jolly boat back to the ship.*

'Give way, handsomely,' she said, squaring her shoulders.

So back to the ship they went, the pinnace, the launch and the jolly boat, with their crews and their surviving officers.

They held a funeral for Forbes at sunset, and Corrie heard the captain say 'We therefore commit this the body of Robert Forbes to the deep, looking for the general Resurrection in the last day, and the life of the world to come.'

She saw Forbes's remains, sewn into a spare hammock and weighted with shot, slide over the side and into a bay that appeared strangely calm and peaceful save for the blazing wrecks of the three coasters. The conflagration, fed by oil from the smashed amphoras, lit up the night sky for miles around, and might burn for days. Off-duty seamen lined the rail to watch the flames, talking to one another in low voices.

After supper, Corrie and Jim joined them.

'So large a fire may attract unwelcome attention from far out in the bay,' said Jim, as they stood gazing at the spectacle.

'I would say the captain is counting on that,' Corrie replied quietly.

'Moth to a flame? The *Tonnerre*? Frigate Captain Jean-Pierre Troude?'

Corrie nodded. 'One look at that blaze and Troude will know where to find us. Unfortunately, thanks to my bringing us in here in the morning mist, we are trapped here in this cove. Our only way of escape is the way we came in, past the guns of Fort Royal, and now that there is no more mist to hide us, the gunners up there in the fort will sink us in short order if we attempt to leave.'

'I can see a vessel entering the strait now. She's too small to be Troude's three-decker, but the fort is not firing at her,' said Jim. 'I wonder why not?'

Mikkel Jensen was standing near them, and answered Jim's query. The big Dane turned and said 'Fort not fire because ship fly flag of my country. Danmark. My country neutral, not fight.'

'You know this ship?' Corrie asked.

'Frigate *Havfruen*. Captain Swarbrek. He sell food and wine to fort. He come here many time. Fort know him. I know him. Hard man, Swarbeck, fond of his wine.'

'The *Havfruen* is about our size,' said Corrie, thoughtfully, and an idea sprang into her mind.

I think there may be a way to save us from being pounded to pieces by the guns of the fort. I had better explore the possibilities.

She took a deep breath. 'Mr. Jensen, a word with you.' She led the Dane away from the crowd and spoke to him in private. She gave him the gist of her idea.

Mikkel Jensen burst out laughing. He slapped his thigh. He bent over, for a moment too weak to stand up straight, then recovered himself somewhat and stared at Corrie, only to start laughing again at the thought of doing what she proposed. He nodded. '*Ja, ja*. Is good. I pay back those Frenchman who sank my *Bardo*.'

Corrie smiled. It was dark now and growing

darker. There was no time to waste. Would Captain Redburn approve her plan? 'Come along, Jensen. Let's see what the captain thinks of the idea.'

The captain was on the quarterdeck discussing the situation with his first lieutenant, Mr. Keeper, Mr. Hartnell, the purser, and the Captain of the Maintop, Billy Brown.

Corrie saluted and explained what she had in mind, Captain Redburn turned to Mikkel Jensen.

'Can you act the part? Of course you can. You were a skipper before the war, as I recall. We'll have to dress you up. First rate idea, Mr. Midshipman Harriman. Take our master-at-arms here to Anne Keeper. See if she can find him some suitable clothes. Is that all right with you, Mr. Keeper?'

'I have a coat with a high collar, broad lapels and a double row of buttons down the front. My wife will be able to find it. I think it might fit.'

'Good. Mr. Hartnell, you are to disguise the ship. Have we enough paint?'

Mr. Hartnell pursed his lips. *If mine had been the Painter's hand, to express what then I saw.* Yes, sir, brown paint I have in abundance, and planks for the men to sit on while they slap it on. In the dark, I presume. And brushes? I do believe we have several different sizes. Consider the task done, sir, within an hour or two.' The purser adjusted the lenses perched upon his nose, and hurried below, shouting for his assistants.

The captain turned to captain of the maintop. 'Billy? We need our rig to look Danish.'

'No worry. My maintop men, we take down topmasts. I be needing the jeers.'

'Help yourself to whatever you need. Can your men take down the topmasts in the dark?'

'My men they sees better in the dark.'

'Put them to work, then, and keep them quiet. Sound carries over water. We don't want the French up there in the fort to hear anything unusual.'

Billy Brown knuckled her forehead by way of acknowledgement, and left the quarterdeck, while Corrie, thrilled that the captain was acting upon her idea, and anxious to lose no time, led Mikkel Jensen aft and knocked on the door of the First Lieutenant's cabin.

'Yes?' said a voice.

The White Lady! I'm going to meet the White Lady.

The first lieutenant's wife, Anne Keeper, opened the door. She was getting ready for bed. Her untrammeled fair hair cascaded in waves about her smooth, rounded shoulders. The hands that held the door were long and slender. The White Lady had dazzling white teeth, eyes with a glint of gold, and skin like cream with floating rose petals.

I feel her influence. I can hardly speak. She has grey eyes, like the goddess Athena.

Corrie cleared her throat and said warily 'I am sorry to disturb you, Mrs. Keeper. The captain begs your help. We are to dress up Mr. Jensen here to look like a Danish captain. Your husband has suggested lending Mr. Jensen a high-collared coat of his, the one with the buttons?'

'Come in, gentlemen,' said Anne Keeper. 'Come

into my cabin. I have the coat here hanging upon this rack. What do you have in mind to do, Mr. Jensen?'

'I am to make like I am Swarbrek, m'am. We'll need a Danish flag, too, with white cross on red, with thin stripe, offset to hoist.'

'You shall have your flag and your coat, Mr. Jensen,' Anne Keeper said, and helped the big man on with the coat. As she did so, she gave a hand signal to Norah, the laundress, who stood by the door.

Norah left in a hurry.

'A bit tight around the chest, but good enough to fool the French, I would say,' the White Lady went on, looking the Dane over carefully. 'What say you, Mr. Midshipman Harriman?'

'Something is not quite right,' said Corrie, cocking her head sideways to have better look. 'He needs a hat. A Danish skipper would have a hat, in this weather.'

'How about this?' Anne Keeper suggested, and set her husband's old tricorn on Mr. Jensen's head. 'Look at yourself in my glass, Mr. Jensen. Do you look like a Danish captain?'

'I *am* Danish captain,' said Jensen, buttoning the coat while regarding his reflection in the White Lady's mirror. He adjusted the three-sided hat until he was satisfied. 'I go now,' he said, and, stooping low, stepped from the cabin, holding the borrowed hat in place with one hand lest the wind should carry it off.

Corrie would have followed him out, but the White Lady put a hand on her arm. 'Stay, Mr. Harriman, if you please,' she said. 'Can you can spare a few minutes?'

'Of course,' said Corrie, and stayed, wondering what Anne Keeper had to say.

Corrie felt a little faint. For the first time, she was alone with the White Lady. Corrie felt the small hairs on the back of her neck rise.

Anne Keeper gives me goose bumps. She holds sway over me. I can feel her power. There is something about this woman. I do not think I should be alone with her. What will the crew think?

The White Lady delved in a drawer, chose an item from a little box she kept there, and handed a neatly sewn cotton pad stuffed with oakum to Corrie. 'For the Moon,' she said.

For the Moon! I'm so embarrassed.

Corrie slipped the soft pad into a pocket of her uniform jacket, and said a silent prayer of thanks.

It's almost my time! How did she know?

Corrie raised her eyebrows.

'On a ship this crowded,' Anne Keeper replied to her unasked question, 'the Moon comes for all of us women at the same time. We women are one. We work together and we live together. You ache for Tomlinson. You saw her die.'

I am frightened. The White Lady knows things I do not know.

'Tomlinson was one of us?' Corrie asked. 'Tomlinson was a woman?'

'Yes, she was. How does that make you feel?'

'Empty,' Corrie replied. 'Cold.' She shivered.

'May I?' The White Lady placed her fingertips lightly on Corrie's brow. 'The fear you feel is no ordinary fear, I see. You fear for the world, and not for yourself. You saved my husband.' The White Lady withdrew her hand and stepped back.

The White Lady pressed her hands together, palm to palm and regarded Corrie solemnly with her fathomless golden eyes. 'What are you, Corrie Harriman?' she asked gently.

It was an odd question, and one that Corrie had never been asked before. The question was not "Who are you?" but "What are you?" and Corrie was not at all sure she knew how to answer. She knew only that she had to give this strange White Lady the truth. There could be no prevarication. One could not lie to the White Lady. Corrie turned to the mirror and gazed at her own reflection. A young, male sea officer looked back at her, with white patches on his uniform.

'I am not what I appear to be,' she answered faintly, touching her own cheeks, and groping in her mind for the frightened child she had been at the dawn of her consciousness, the child who had fought the terrifying invisible wetness that had threatened to smother her. 'I am nobody,' she said, astonished.

The White Lady nodded. 'You are all the women who have ever been and all who shall follow after. You are creator, nurturer and destroyer. You think you voyage in search of your mother, Corrie, but look in the glass. Your mother is here.'

Corrie stared wide-eyed at the White Lady.

'No, I am not your mother. That is not what I mean. You are your mother. Look at your reflection in my glass and see your mother in yourself. She is you.

You are her. We are all mothers reborn, and more.'

Corrie shook her head. 'What I see in your glass is not my mother but a strange man called Mr. Midshipman Harriman,' said Corrie. 'I hardly know my mother, to be honest. She was seldom there for me.'

'She was always there for you. Look in the mirror again. Yes, the sailors see Mr. Midshipman Harriman, but you and I see the *truth*. We are not attending a masked ball, Corrie, and this war we are fighting is no joke, believe me. We have to bring down Joséphine, that's what we women have to do.'

Corrie laughed. 'We have to bring down Napoleon Bonaparte, you mean,' she said. 'It is Napoleon we are fighting.'

'The men would like you to believe that we are fighting Napoleon,' said the White Lady. 'Men think they can win wars by blowing things up. No, Joséphine Bonaparte is is our real enemy, so we are doctoring her *petit pains*.'

'We are?' said Corrie, raising her eyebrows.

The White Lady is nuts. But there is something about her I can't put my finger on. She gives off an aura of far-reaching power, and I find her confidence inspiring. She has a look in her eyes that gives me hope.

XVI

'WE women are preventing Joséphine from having a baby,' the White Lady explained, 'while striving to make the poor girl think she is being poisoned by agents of the Grand Duke Alexander Pavlovich. Soon we shall arrange for her to be sent into exile.'

'When you say "our" and "we" of whom are you speaking?' Corrie asked warily.

'I am speaking of you and I, Corrie, and of all the other women in the world,' the White Lady answered, and paused to look at her critically. 'You do know that we women are all over the world?'

'Well, yes, I suppose we are, but I have never thought of us all working together, nor have I seen any sign that we are doing so. Is this a revolutionary notion? Have you been reading the writings of Olympe de Gouge?'

The White Lady raised a slender white hand and said '*A woman has the right to be executed but she also has the right to become a Minister of State.* I hope you agree? I hope you are familiar with all of de Gouge's writings? She was an inspiration to women everywhere. The men cut off her head, but they could not silence her.'

'Olympe de Gouge is *dead*?' This was news to Corrie.

'Yes, she is. The men held a trial. They quoted a line spoken by a character in one of her plays, and then, regarding that line as her own view of the matter, executed her.'

'I'm sorry.'

'I, too, was sorry, when the news first reached me. We need all our best women just now. You have a brain, Corrie Harriman, and you read books. I am glad. If this wild scheme of yours involving Jensen works, and we manage somehow to escape from the guns of Fort Royal, what shall we women have Captain Redburn do next?'

Corrie stiffened. 'Mrs. Keeper, I have no plans to *have* our captain to do anything. I am a mere midshipman, but recently appointed, and it is not my place to tell my captain what to do.'

'You are a *woman*,' said the White Lady, beating her fist into her palm. 'Try to think like one. Answer my question.'

Corrie stared at the White Lady's gleaming shoulder and her tumbling golden locks that stirred in the candlelight with every sway of the ship. Visible through the gun port, the reflections of the lights burning on Castle Hill danced in the waves. The French soldiers were awake up there on the mount, keeping a close watch on the *Swift* lest she slip past them in the dark.

'We should encourage the captain to find Troude,' said Corrie.

'Why?' asked the White Lady. 'Troude's ship, the *Tonnerre*, has twice our number of guns and his guns can fire four times our weight in metal. We should all be killed.'

'Not necessarily,' said Corrie. 'There may be a way to bring Troude down, and that should be our aim.

If we sink the *Tonnerre*, Troude will be unable to protect the French supply ships, the men in the fort will grow weak from lack of food, and the men manning the battery at St. Pierre will go hungry, and the French hope of re-establishing New France will begin to founder.'

'Well, well,' said the White Lady. 'We wonder what to make of you, Mr. Midshipman Harriman. 'You are a strong woman, and strong women have enemies. Collins, Samuelson and Wicks run the gambling games in the forecastle, and blame you for Sly's dismissal and incarceration. I should keep your eyes open and watch your back, if I were you. You do have a few friends in the galley, and old Harbottle is on your side, for one, and the story of your knocking the captain of the *Galatée* into the sea has spread like wildfire through the lower deck, but you must remember that men are fickle. Today's hero is tomorrow's scapegoat. Men *talk*.'

Corrie nodded. She could hear men talking outside the port. She heard also a rattle of cans, and then the squeal of a pulley. In obedience to orders that had been given as a result of her suggestion to the captain, those men were forfeiting precious hours in their hammocks to paint over the yellow and black Nelson chequer of the *Swift*'s sides, and to apply instead a uniform coat of drab brown. Could they make the *Swift* appear like a foreign vessel by dawn? She hoped so. Then there was the matter of that Danish flag they would need. 'Do you need my help cutting out the pieces for the flag, Mrs. Keeper?'

The White Lady smiled. 'Norah and Gladys are

making the flag. Go and do something more useful, Mr. Midshipman Harriman. Rehearse Jensen in his part.'

'Yes, Mrs. Keeper,' said Corrie, and left the White Lady's cabin more confused that she had entered it.

The White Lady can read my mind. The White Lady brings the Moon. The White Lady says Tomlinson was a girl.

Tomlinson was a girl.

I am ashamed. I couldn't look at Tomlinson's body. I turned away. I didn't know. I'm sorry for her.

Corrie helped Jensen rehearse his part. The night wore on. Towards dawn, she found the companionway barred by a press of seamen and officers. She bumped into the First Lieutenant. 'What's going on here, Mr. Keeper?' she asked.

'Captain's orders. Nobody is to show their faces on deck except the master-at-arms and a handful of seamen, no more men on deck than Captain Swarbrek would have to do his bidding in that frigate of his, the *Havfruen*. The *Swift* has been painted to look just like the *Havfruen*.'

'I'm glad to hear it. Are we leaving the bay yet? Is there a morning mist?'

'Yes, we are leaving, and yes, there is quite a lot of mist.' He put his head above the deck for a quick peep. 'I can barely make out the fort.'

'That's good,' said Corrie. 'With luck,' she went on hopefully, 'the gunners up in the fort won't see the real *Havfruen* for the mist. If they do, they will smell a rat.'

The first lieutenant regarded Corrie with suspicion.

'This was all your idea, wasn't it? Dressing our master-at-arms up as Swarbrek, and taking down the topmasts to alter our silhouette?'

'If I am to blame, sir, I should be blamed for bringing us into the bay in the first place to deal with those coasters, and trapping us here. It is our captain who is bringing us out, and the decision to take down the topmasts and to repaint the ship were his decisions, I assure you. Are we in range of the fort?'

'Just about. Listen. Somebody up on the heights is ringing a bell. We have been been spotted. Now I suppose the question is: Will our disguised ship fool them? Will they withhold their fire? I do hope they can see the Danish flag flying from our jack.' Keeper peeped over the top of the combing again. 'They are not firing at us yet.'

'They do not wish to sink their supply ship,' said Corrie. 'They think Jensen is Swarbrek, and the *Swift* is the *Havfruen*. We may have fooled them, sir.'

'I hope we have,' said Keeper, ducking his head down again. 'If they do start firing and we have to make a run for it, at least we'll have this offshore breeze to help us out, but we shan't be able to set any topsails. I hate having to skulk below the deck like this. I'd far rather be by the wheel where I can see what's going on.'

'I, too, should like to be up on deck,' said Corrie. 'I feel a change in the swells, sir. I think we are passing the headland. The wind out in the Bay of Plaisance must be easterly.'

Keeper nodded. 'I feel it. We are sailing out into

the wider waters and leaving the fort behind.' He took another peep. 'Yes, I think we are going to get away with our little deception. I can't see the fort anymore. Castle Hill is cloaked by the mist. Come on!' cried Keeper, and jumped up onto the deck. He looked about him eagerly. 'We might start the men replacing those topmasts.'

'I'd advise against doing that right away,' said Corrie, clambering up onto the deck to join the first lieutenant. 'May I respectfully suggest that we stay in disguise for the time being? Those coasters are still burning, and Troude may be coming to investigate the blaze, sir.'

'Troude? That French fellow the captain is always going on about? That Frigate Captain, Jean-Pierre Troude? What makes you think he's in the offing?'

'He'll be looking for us, sir. His task is to re-establish New France here in Plaisance, and we are the only English warship with enough guns to thwart his plan. His first priority must be to destroy us.'

'Deck, there!' called down Brown from the maintop.

'What do you see, Billy?' asked Corrie, looking up.

'We in trouble,' shouted Brown.

'What kind of trouble?'

'Dutty Duppy Man trouble.'

'An enemy ship? Are you sure? Whereaway?'

'Hull down to windward and fine on the port bow.'

'Tom, the spyglass!' Corrie clambered up the ratlines with the telescope to have a proper look. Dawn had turned the grey sea blue, and porpoises were arching their backs as they leapt from the water, but Corrie had an eye only for that distant sail.

She fiddled with the lenses until the inverted image leapt into focus. The strange sail was a battleship and it was flying the flag of the revolution.

Corrie made her way back down to the deck as fast as she could, saluted the captain, and said 'I think she may be the *Tonnerre*, sir, coming down on us fast with a freshening wind behind her.'

'Lend me your glass,' said Captain Redburn, and peered at the approaching vessel. 'You are correct. I recognize that patched forecourse. She's the *Tonnerre* all right. A third-rate. She has eighty guns and may blow us apart with a single broadside.'

'If we were close alongside her, sir,' said Corrie, greatly daring, 'she might not be able to hurt us at all.'

'Explain,' barked the captain, his eye still on his enemy.

'That book you lent me, sir, speaks of the "arc of fire." The *Tonnerre* is a Third-Rate, with two gun decks, while our *Swift* is a Sixth-Rate. Were we to lay our *Swift* alongside the *Tonnerre*, then Troude might find himself unable to fire upon our hull at all, for no matter how hard he depressed his guns, the shot from the *Tonnerre*'s guns would pass clear over our heads and into the sea, while we, tucked away safely under the *Tonnerre*'s "arc of fire", might batter his ship to pieces with impunity. The book could be wrong, sir.'

The captain closed the telescope with a click and looked at Corrie. 'I like the idea, but there's one snag.

How are we to come that close to the *Tonnerre* without being shot to pieces during our approach?'

'We look like the Dane, sir. We look like the Captain Swarbrek's ship. We have painted the name "HAVFRUEN" on our transom. Troude will know of the *Havfruen*, and will think we have just delivered his wine to Fort Royal. What could be more natural than that he should meet the *Havfruen* here, leaving the protection of the fort? We could offer him some wine. He'll know we can't possibly be his enemy, or he would have heard the fort firing at us. And he'll want to know what has been lighting up the night sky, sir. He'll want to know about those burning coasters.'

'Yes,' said the captain, rubbing his jaw. 'I see what you mean. We might fool him. On the other hand, we must be careful not to contravene the rules of war. Sooner or later that Danish flag will have to be hauled down, and our own flag raised in its place.'

'Yes, sir,' said Corrie. 'We could leave that until the very last moment, sir, and open fire at point blank range,' said Corrie. 'We should have no trouble hitting his hull.'

'Mr. Keeper. What do you think of this scheme of Harriman's?'

'Risky, sir. But if we can offset the disadvantage of the *Tonnerre*'s superior firepower by doing what Harriman suggests, then I think it might be worth the risk. In my opinion, sir.'

The captain handed the spyglass to young Fraser and stood for a moment, his hands clasped behind his back, balancing the odds of the engagement.

He made up his mind. 'We'll try it. Get back down below, all of you. Tell the Marines to lie down in the cable tier. I don't want the enemy to see their scarlet uniforms. Helm, bring us to the wind. We shall wait for the *Tonnerre* to come down to us. Mr. Jensen, how good is your French?'

'Passable, captain.'

'Here's what I want you to say…' The captain spoke quietly to Jensen, and then raised his voice to say 'Rawlinson, Peckham, this is no time for sightseeing. Break out the arm's chest. Quietly. A weapon for every man. No talking. Sergeant Deering, when you have seen to your men, I'd be grateful if you would go down to the brig and unshackle the prisoner. Make sure he has a weapon to fight with if we are boarded.'

If the *Swift* were to be boarded by Frenchmen, as seemed likely, the captain did not want Augustus Sly to die chained to the deck without having a chance to defend himself. She hoped she could trust Deering to provide Sly with a better weapon than the one Sly had foisted on her brother for the cutting out of the *Galatée*.

Speaking of Jim, here he was, striding along the gun deck and buckling on a two-handed short sword.

'Arc of fire?' he asked her, remembering her account of the book she had been reading.

She nodded. 'It's risky. One well-aimed broadside from Troude and we're done for.'

Jim pulled the buckle tight and adjusted the sword at his hip. 'But if we come close alongside her, the day will be ours?' he asked.

'I hope so. Did you finish reading that *Gunnery*

Manual by Robert Wilson?'

'I read it twice. I have to remember to prick the cartridge. If I shan't be using the coigns to elevate the guns, then I just keep firing away as quickly as I can.'

'Good.' She lowered her voice. 'I hope I don't get us all killed.'

Jim grinned. 'You'd better not. I want to live to be an officer.'

'You shall, I promise,' said Corrie. 'Don't trip over that sword.'

'I'll be careful,' said Jim, and he followed Billy Brown and others into the rigging.

With the stiff breeze behind her, and a full set of sails drawing, the French ship *Tonnerre* came tearing down upon the waiting *Swift*.

Corrie could see the enemy ship's bow cleaving the waves. As the three-decker came closer, and the gap between the two ships narrowed, Corrie began to make out the pale faces of the French crew, studying what they took to be a Danish supply vessel.

Corrie noticed that not all the members of the French crew were from France. They hailed from many parts of the world, just as the *Swift's* crew did.

She could see African faces, Caribbean faces and Arab faces among those peering down from the *Tonnerre*'s tops, and from her gun ports, and had to wonder what this war was really about, when so many of the sailors involved in the fighting had only the vaguest notion of why the war was being fought, and many were more interested in winning than in preserving the divine right of kings and queens to rule or creating a new world for the sake of liberty, fraternity and equality.

Now the *Tonnerre* was very close indeed, and in a position to blow the *Swift* out of the water. Corrie narrowed her eyes. Was that Jean-Pierre Troude, the enemy captain, that resplendent figure she could see on the quarterdeck, wearing his hat cross-wise? He had a spyglass in his hand. She hoped Troude would not use that glass, not until the two ships lay side by side like two peas in a pod. There were many English particulars to the *Swift*'s rig that might give her away if examined too closely.

The *Tonnerre* swung around under their stern and drew alongside in their lee. As she drifted to within musket range, Corrie saw dozens of her men run out along her yards and take in her sails. She watched this operation with a professional eye, noting that the French crew was not as efficient as Billy Brown's.

A shadow fell over the ship. The huge cambered side of the French man-of-war towered over them, blocking out the sun and stilling the wind.

From her hiding place in the shadow of the companionway, Corrie craned her neck and gazed upward in awe at the two tiers of her guns. She saw the faces of the French gun crews staring down at her. Her heart raced. If those Frenchmen fired those huge forty-pounders of theirs, then she might never again dance at the Crown and Anchor; nor solve the aching mystery of her absent parents, nor read in Homer's thrilling tales of the grey-eyed goddess Pallas Athena who appeared to warriors in time of peril.

XVII

A STENTORIAN voice from above cried '*Qui êtes-vous?*'

Corrie had no doubt that this was the voice of the French Frigate Captain, Jean-Pierre Troude. She could see his imposing figure high above her, silhouetted against the snowy white canvas of the *Tonnerre*'s mainsail. Troude was standing on the main deck of his ship, resplendent in a huge Napoleonic hat and a striped topcoat with a high collar. He was addressing them by means of a speaking trumpet that gave his voice a measured cadence.

'*Qui... êtes...vous?*'

Corrie was apprehensive.

I hope Mikkel Jensen says the right thing in reply. I hope his French is better than his English.

The disguised Jensen, looking every bit the part of a Danish captain in Mr. Keeper's coat and hat, answered the hail. He said he was the Danish skipper Swarbrek. He said something cheerful and short in Danish, and then spoke at greater length in French. Corrie heard him speak of a case of wine for the good captain, and of sharing a cup together for the amity of nations.

While Corrie understood the gist of what Jensen was saying, she was not sure that Troude would be fooled by the Dane's patter. Jensen sounded a little too glib, and a little too matter-of-fact for a skipper facing all those gaping gun ports.

Troude had his spyglass to his eye now and was

peering down at the drab brown ship that was rising and falling with the swells beside his own. Was he suspicious? Had he met the real captain Swarbrek on a previous occasion? Had he realized that Jensen was an imposter?

Corrie could feel the shock transmitted through the deck to her feet as the two vessels, moving uneasily in the heaving seas, scraped against one another. Corrie was frustrated.

We are under the French arc of fire. What's Captain Redburn waiting for? He must engage the enemy without wasting a moment. We have to catch Troude by surprise.

Troude was looking over the disguised *Swift* inch by inch. He stared long and hard at the brand new Danish flag. Corrie wondered if he would spot the English frapping on the falls, or read the English lettering on the compass card. They were losing precious moments.

She whispered in Captain Redburn's ear. 'This is our chance to give him a broadside, sir. We should open fire right now.'

'We are not flying our flag, Midshipman Harriman. Even war has its niceties.'

'With all due respect, sir, the flag doesn't matter. If the *Tonnerre* fires first, she may damage our rigging, captain.'

Corrie held her breath.

This was my idea. What was I thinking of? Jim is up in there in the maintop. If the Tonnerre *does fire, he may be the first to die.*

'Shall I pass the word to the gun decks, captain?' she asked softly, trying to coax Redburn into taking action. The minutes were ticking away, and disaster loomed.

Corrie was all too aware of the cries of seabirds, and of the dull roar of surf. The wind must be carrying both ships toward the land. She and the captain were hiding beneath the companionway steps. She dared not raise her head to confirm her suspicion, lest Troude should spot her, but if she were hearing the waves breaking on those twisted pillars of rock that stood out from the towering cliffs, then she feared that both ships would soon be in trouble, and time was running out fast both for Troude and for Captain Redburn.

'Sir?' Corrie put her fist before her face and bit down on her knuckles.

Hurry up and make up your mind, captain. The suspense is killing me.

The bawling of the seabirds grew louder, and the rumble of the surf more alarming. Corrie ran out of patience. She pushed forward through the press of sailors who were doing their best to keep out of sight of the French.

'Clear a path,' she said, firmly. 'I have to speak to the first lieutenant.'

'We're all going to die,' said Campbell. 'The captain's gone doolally.'

'You'll be the first to die, Campbell, if you don't get out of my way. Step aside, I say!'

Campbell stepped aside, and Corrie found Mr. Keeper crouching by the steerage hatch, peering up into the chains of the *Tonnerre*.

Corrie threw formalities to the wind and grabbed the first lieutenant by the arm. 'Mr. Keeper,' she said fiercely in his ear. 'We're in position. This is our one and only chance. The French can't depress their guns far enough to reach our hull. We should open fire. If we don't we shall be swept onto the rocks.'

'We are still flying the Danish flag, young Harriman. We can't open fire until our own flag goes up. It's the rules of war,' the first lieutenant explained.

'Stop worrying about the rules of war,' said Corrie, hotly, ' and think of your wife. Think of Anne, and of young Fraser. Troude is up there now looking at us through his glass. How long do you think it will take him to figure out that we are English? Not so very long, I'll warrant. Troude doesn't care a fig for the rules of war. Ask Mikkel Jensen what happened to his ship the *Bardo*. She was flying the Danish flag when she was attacked. Are we going to wait for Troude to make the first move? We have to act. Surprise is half the battle. Give the order, I beg you.'

Mr. Keeper gazed thoughtfully at Corrie. 'You're quite the firebrand, Mr. Harriman.'

'Sir, it was my idea to bring the *Swift* this close to the *Tonnerre*. Being this close gives us an advantage, but we stand to lose that advantage if we do not act at once. Sir.'

Mr. Keeper sighed. 'Very well, then. Come along with me, Harriman, and we'll try to persuade the captain together.'

Fuming, Corrie followed the first lieutenant back

through the throng. Every second's delay increased the danger to her brother, to Billy Brown, and to all of the other maintop men up aloft. When the *Tonnerre* let loose her barrage, her rounds might not find the hull of the *Swift* but they would cause havoc in her rigging. Corrie clenched her fists.

It'll be my fault if Jim is killed. If I were in charge, I'd have given the order to fire three minutes ago. This is frustrating.

'Captain Redburn?' said Keeper. 'Our midshipman here thinks it's time we fired on the *Tonnerre*.'

'Yes,' said the captain. 'I have just sent your boy Fraser to the jackstaff to take down the Danish ensign and to hoist our own,' the captain replied. 'As soon as we have our proper flag flying, we'll begin.'

Greatly daring, Corrie leaned forward and spoke in an urgent whisper. 'I don't think we can wait until then, captain. The *Tonnerre* is headreaching on us, and we are on a lee shore. There's a big underwater reef near here that we skirted by on our way into the bay. I saw the coral clearly. Troude is growing suspicious. I don't think he believes Jensen's story. In my opinion, we should do well to start our attack at once.'

'I commend your zeal, Mr. Harriman,' said the captain, 'but it would be ungentlemanly of us to fire under false pretenses. There you are! The boy has reached the flag halyard and is lowering the Danish splitflag. Now I think it is time we officers made our way to the quarterdeck. Come with me and we'll show Troude and his crew how true Englishmen behave when danger threatens.'

Her heart in her mouth, Corrie followed the captain and the first lieutenant onto the quarterdeck. 'This is not what I planned,' she said. 'This was supposed to be a surprise. Sending the boy to lower the flag has placed us all in peril.'

'War is a perilous business, Mr. Harriman, and I advise you to respect your elders and not berate them.'

'I am most dreadfully sorry, sir,' said Corrie. 'I spoke out of turn. I can only hope you will overlook my outburst.'

A sea cave boomed. The cries of the seabirds became hysterical.

'You are not Swarbrek,' said the voice of Frigate Captain Jean-Pierre Troude magnified by his speaking trumpet, 'and your ship is not the *Havfruen*.' Corrie heard the snap as the Frenchman closed his telescope decisively. Troude turned and spoke sharply to his aide.

Corrie heard the order to fire being shouted from deck to deck of the *Tonnerre*.

Moments later, explosions too loud to bear split the air. Balls howled overhead. An enemy shot slammed into the foremast sending splinters flying. 'Run up our flag!' shouted Captain Redburn. 'Marines! Show yourselves! Man the side.'

Corrie could not believe what she was hearing. It was not the Marines that were needed to counter this attack, but the *Swift*'s big guns.

Give the order to fire, captain!

The maintop platform of the *Swift* was hit. Yards and sails, blocks and tackle, came raining down on the deck.

A falling yard struck down the captain. The massive timber slewed across the deck, missing Corrie by inches, and slammed the first lieutenant, sending him flying into the mainmast.

Corrie ran to help.

Anne Keeper was already at her husband's side, his hand in hers. 'Arthur?' she said. 'Arthur. It's me, Anne.'

Mr. Keeper's staring eyes, and the strange angle of his head to his body, told Corrie all she needed to know. The first lieutenant was dead.

'It's no good, Anne. He's gone,' Corrie said. 'I'm sorry. Better go and see to Fraser.'

'No!' said Anne Keeper, tears streaming down her cheeks. 'No!' She would not let go of her husband's limp hand. She began to shake.

Corrie gave the White Lady's arm a squeeze. 'I have to go,' she said, and leapt over the fallen blocks and cordage.

Corrie had a sinking feeling. She feared the worst.

Where's the captain? I must find the captain.

The captain was badly injured. The falling spar had crushed his rib cage. It was hard for him to speak. He was bleeding from his mouth.

'Mr. Keeper,' the captain said, hoarsely. 'Is he all right?'

Corrie shook her head. 'He's dead,' she said.

'Dear heaven!' exclaimed Redburn, and Corrie saw the despair in his eyes. Then she saw the captain make one last effort.

'Tell Mr. Weevil you're the captain, now,' said

Redburn, speaking his words carefully and slowly.

'Sir?' Corrie froze. She could not believe what she was hearing.

'I'm promoting you to captain,' said Redburn. 'You're in charge of the ship now. The *Swift* is all… yours…'

The life went out of Redburn's eyes.

Oh, my God. He has died. They are both dead, and I'm the only officer left alive. Mr. Weevil is the ship's Master, but his job is merely to advise the captain.

A series of explosions rocked the *Swift* as the *Tonnerre* fired again, knocking away the *Swift*'s bowsprit and smashing her jolly boat to shards. A score of shot holes appeared in her sails, but not one of those balls struck the *Swift*'s hull, so far as Corrie could tell. In that respect, at least, her plan was working.

A feeling of anger greater than any she had known seized Corrie.

We must fire back, and we have to fire back now. No more delays. I need Jim. I can't do this alone.

She cupped her hands around her mouth and shouted up at the smashed-in maintop platform. 'Billy, I need Jim.'

'I send that man down,' Billy Brown shouted back from her half-ruined platform.

Hurry, Jim. We're nearly on the rocks.

Her brother came sliding down a backstay and landed on the deck. He seemed unhurt.

Thank heavens.

'Jim. I'm over here!'

When her brother jumped over the wreckage of the

sprung yard, and saw the two bodies of the ship's senior officers, his jaw dropped. 'They're both dead?' he said. 'The captain *and* the first lieutenant? Who is in charge?'

'I am,' Corrie replied. 'Redburn has made me captain, and I'm making you first lieutenant. It's up to you and me, now, Jim.'

'You're making me first lieutenant of the *Swift*? We're under fire. What am I supposed to do?'

'Remember that gunnery manual?'

Jim nodded, staring at his sister as if looking at a stranger.

'I want you to fire our guns at the *Tonnerre*'s rudder. I want you to blow the *Tonnerre*'s rudder to pieces. Can you do that?'

Jim nodded eagerly. 'I'll double shot the guns.'

'Hurry! Troude will be boarding soon.'

'Aye aye, captain,' said Jim, and hurried below, shouting orders to the crews of the guns.

Corrie felt a burst of hope.

Good for Jim.

Moments later, the deck shook under Corrie's feet as the *Swift*'s guns discharged and recoiled, pounding the lower deck of the *Tonnerre* and smashing holes in her orlop and in her fore cockpit.

A pig squealed and a frightened steer bellowed.

'Well done, Jim!' she shouted. 'We are returning fire at last. Now reload those guns and disable the *Tonnerre*'s rudder. I'm counting on you.'

Mr. Weevil appeared, walking unsteadily out of a cloud of blue powder smoke. He looked about him in a puzzled fashion.

'Mr. Weevil,' said Corrie, quickly. 'We are going to need our topmasts back in place. I'd be grateful if you would find some hands and put them to work.

Mr. Weevil dug the chronometer from his fob pocket and peered down at his timepiece. 'Sunset will be at seventeen minutes past six,' he said gravely.

Corrie grabbed Mr. Weevil by his shoulders and shook him. 'Mr. Weevil! Wake up! The captain and the first lieutenant are dead. I'm in command. We're in the middle of a fight. Here's the master-at-arms, Mr. Jensen. We're going to need topsails, and we're going to need them soon. Those topmasts we struck to disguise our silhouette must be returned to where they came from, starting with the foretopmast. Take as many hands as you need and get the job done.'

'Maybe too late for that,' said Jensen, looking over her shoulder. 'I think those no-good French seamen want to board us.'

'Leave the French to me, and do as I say.'

'*Ja*, my captain,' said Jensen, and began shouting names. 'Smith! Evans! Portman! Come here! I have work for you.'

Corrie felt a thrill of excitement. The Dane had called her 'captain' and was obeying her order.

There is hope for us yet.

Corrie could see that the *Tonnerre* was moving slightly faster through the breakers than the *Swift*, and was overtaking the smaller vessel by degrees. Corrie watched aghast as Frigate Captain Troude led a party of armed French seamen aft along the *Tonnerre*'s side.

She saw Troude leap up onto the bulwarks. She heard him shout something to his sailors, who answered him with an angry yell.

Corrie blanched. Events were moving faster than she had expected. Perhaps she was not cut out to be a captain.

They are going to board us this very instant. How can we stop them? I'm not sure we can.

Then Corrie remembered how she had fallen from the sky like an avenging angel upon the unfortunate captain of the *Galatée* and knocked that poor man over the side and into the sea.

'Billy!' she shouted up at the maintop. 'We're being boarded. Bring your maintop men down here! Fast!'

Troude sprang aboard, and his sailors were at at his heels, shouting and waving their weapons excitedly.

Corrie remembered just in time the gleaming weapon that she had taken from the captain of the *Galatée*. She drew that blade from its scabbard, and turned to face the French boarders, her sword in her hand.

XVIII

DOWN they came, Billy Brown and her maintop men, falling from their shattered platform like so many monkeys leaping from a tree. They slammed into the boarding Frenchman and sent them flying.

The *Swift*'s seamen and marines joined the fight. One brawny seaman laid about him with an axe. But more and more of Troude's sailors and soldiers came pouring into the *Swift*.

Corrie froze. There was no mistaking that cruel, haughty face under that absurd Napoleonic hat. Frigate Captain Jean-Pierre Troude was on the move, making for the *Swift*'s quarterdeck to kill her captain.

Troude is headed straight for me. He doesn't know I am the captain. He thinks I'm just a midshipman. I must stand my ground.

Troude doffed his plumed hat mockingly and bowed to the small figure blocking his path. '*En garde!*' he cried, and then lunged suddenly, intending to run his sword through this upstart English midshipman and have done with him.

Corrie bent her knees and deflected Troude's attack with a sharp striking motion, just as her fencing master had taught her to do, and the tactic worked. Troude missed his mark.

Quick as a flash, Troude stamped his foot on the deck to distract her, and launched a second sudden attack, using his rear leg to thrust his erect body forward in a bold and surprising move intended to skewer her.

Corrie kept her blade in contact with his, and managed to deflect this second sally also, but she could feel how strong he was and had to wonder how long she could last.

Another quick jab like that and I'm dead. Re-load those guns, Jim. Hurry. I can't hold off this man forever. He's too strong.

She knew that Jim would be busy in the twilight of the gun deck, telling the captain of the first gun to put his priming wire in the vent and to load the weapon with two cast iron rounds.

'Prick the cartridge through the vent,' her brother would be saying, and watching closely to make sure the gun captain inserted the goose quill filled with fine gunpowder carefully. She knew she could depend on Jim to pay attention to details.

'Run out,' Corrie heard him say, and felt the rumble of gun trucks transmitted through the deck to her feet.

I must distract Troude. I must keep him busy. I don't want him to notice what Jim is up to.

She slid her blade down Troude's forte and made a quick flunge to confuse him.

Alas, her feint was not a success. Troude responded so quickly with a riposte that he drew her around in a complete circle.

Ouch! I didn't see that coming.

Corrie narrowed her eyes. Would Jim be able to disable the French battleship's rudder before Troude ran her through?

He's coming for me again.

'Prybars!' she heard Jim shout, and pictured the back axle of a gun carriage being lifted to slew the gun around. He was aiming the weapon. 'Wedge!' Corrie visualized the quoin being driven home to depress the muzzle. Jim would want the balls to fly downward if they were to shatter the gudgeons upon which the *Tonnerre*'s rudder depended.

In the meanwhile, it was up to her to keep Troude too busy to see the danger to his ship.

It was time for a *pris de fer*.

She made a sweeping action upwards, carrying Troude's blade over her shoulder, and then spun on her heel and struck at Troude's head a resounding blow with her guard.

I hope that hurt. I have to keep Troude's mind off what Jim is doing.

To strike your opponent with your guard was by no means fair, but so long as her blow served to distract Troude from what was going on down below on the gun deck, Corrie did not care if she played foul.

Troude was livid. He had been insulted. His head hurt. Furious, he pushed his chest hard against hers. '*Imbécile!*' he shouted in her face, and spit flew from his mouth.

Grimly Corrie held her ground.

I have his attention. If I can just hold him off a little longer without being killed...

She and Troude were *corps á corps*, and Corrie dared not disengage. She was buying time for her brother. At any moment now the first gun would be in line with the enemy's upper pintle, and her brother would pull the lanyard.

Boom! She heard the gun go off, and then the splintering crash of the rounds hitting the enemy ship. The rudder of the *Tonnerre* exploded.

Troude's face was inches from hers when the discharge of the gun shook the deck. His breath smelled of pig's trotters. Something ripped apart Corrie's uniform coat, slicing away several buttons, and she felt a scorching pain, followed by a welling of blood. She pushed Troude away from her angrily. What had happened? What had he done to her? How had he hurt her?

I'm wounded!

She looked down at her chest and saw a spreading stain of scarlet. Her mind reeled.

Troude broke the rules. He has a hidden blade in his left hand. I must disengage. He has outsmarted me.

She was aghast.

They'll carry me below. They'll take me down to Cook and her knives. The purser will be down there in the twilight sawing off some wretched sailor's leg and reciting poetry. 'And three times to the child I said, "Why, Edward, tell me why?" They'll find out who I really am, down there in the cockpit.

'Keep it up, Jim!' she shouted, stepping back without lowering her guard or taking her eyes from Troude's triumphant, gloating face. She was bleeding profusely, that was true, but she was still in the game. Her enemy might be grinning like a death's head, but Corrie meant to stay on her feet for long enough to see Troude's undoing. It might take several more shots to make that damage to the *Tonnerre*'s rudder irreparable. Her plan was working. She had only to prevent Troude from seeing the danger.

Judging by his expression, Troude was seeing something he had not assumed in Corrie. Where he had expected panic and despair, he saw courage and resolve. He, too, took a step backward. He lowered the point of his sword and stared at her. Something was not right. He was the victor, not she. Unless…?

Corrie could see that she had him puzzled. She saw him gaze at her in alarm and could guess what was passing through Troude's mind. This young man, Troude had to be saying to himself (for he could have no idea that he was fighting a young woman) this young man has been injured and ought to be sinking to his knees and begging me for mercy, but instead he is showing every sign of triumph.

Corrie saw Troude risk a quick glance over his shoulder. She saw the fury on his face when he registered the damage being done to the rudder of his *Tonnerre*. He had been hoodwinked, and now he must hurry back to his ship, and take his boarders back with him. He must steer his ship away from this lee shore. The situation was as clear to him now as it was to Corrie. As the *Tonnerre* slid past the *Swift*, gun after gun would come to bear, and before long the ruin of the *Tonnerre*'s rudder would be complete, and the *Tonnerre* would no longer answer to her helm at all. Troude had no choice but to retreat.

Corrie battled with her own inner misgivings as she stood there, gazing fiercely at Troude. She was conscious of the stain on her white shirt expanding with every gush from her arteries.

I'm the captain, but he doesn't know that. He thinks I'm just a midshipman, and he can't spare the time to finish me off. His ship is in trouble and he has to go. The hidden blade in the left hand! The oldest trick in the book! My fencing master warned me, but I didn't listen.

She felt something trickling down her ribs.

The danger to both vessels was growing by the minute.

She watched Troude back away. She saw his eyes dart to his companions. She heard him shout orders. She saw him turn back to her and she heard him say 'Tell your captain I have not finished with him.'

Troude made a hasty retreat. 'Tell him I shall be back,' he shouted as he thrust his sword back into its sheath, jumped up on the bulwarks, leapt for the *Tonnerre*, and landed in a boarding net hanging from the after cockpit. His boarders tried to follow him, but two missed the net and fell into the sea.

The boarding Frenchmen have returned to their ship to try to save her. Now I shall try to save mine.

Racked with pain, Corrie sheathed her own sword, a simple action that took a prodigious effort, and staggered toward the companionway. She joined her brother. Her blood spotted the deck leaving a trail behind her.

BOOM!

A second gun went off, sounding very loud in the confined space of the gun deck, and two more rounds smashed into the *Tonnerre*'s rudder, causing further damage. Corrie watched the gun recoil, throwing itself backward until brought up sharp by the breeching rope made fast to eyebolts attached to the ship's side. She was pleased that Jim did not wait to supervise the worming, sponging and reloading of that gun but instead ran on to help the crew of the next gun take careful aim at the *Tonnerre*'s rudder.

Corrie peered through the port to assess the damage done to her enemy.

My plan is working.

One by one, the guns of the *Swift* belched flame and smoke. Round after round flew true. The great rudder of the *Tonnerre* was being pounded into wreckage. Without a working rudder, the French would find it hard to steer clear of the reef. They might not even have time to lower their boats before they struck. That was an awful thought. Corrie experienced a wave of dizziness. She grabbed a stanchion for support.

I have to stay alive for a little longer. I have to look after my ship and my crew.

In the battle between the two ships, a moment of truth was approaching. Now that Troude and his boarders had returned to their own vessel, the *Tonnerre* would resume firing.

'Join me on the quarterdeck as soon as you're done, Jim,' she shouted.

'Aye aye, sir,' Jim shouted back. He was too intent on his gunnery to notice that his sister was hurt.

Returning slowly to the upper deck Corrie met with a working party of seamen lugging a heavy roll of storm sail up through the main hatch.

'That sail is our best hope for making our escape,' she said. 'Bend it on, quickly.'

'Aye aye, captain,' said ordinary seaman Campbell and he gave the huge roll a shove. As the fresh canvas unrolled across the deck, Corrie was surprised to see emerging from the innermost folds of the roll that despicable prisoner and one-time master-at-arms, Augustus Sly.

'Come on!' cried Campbell, his eyes as wide as saucers. 'Hiding in the roll, were you? Thought you'd be safe, did you?'

'Master-of-Rats is wot he is,' said another.

'None of your lip,' said Sly, scrambling to his feet. 'Got my reasons. See? Had to save the ship.'

'Had to save your hide, you mean, you bampot,' said Campbell.

'Don't you call me names,' said Sly.

'We haven't time for this,' said Corrie. 'Stand aside, Sly, and let these men get to work. I want this topsail set.'

As if to emphasize the urgency of Corrie's words, the guns of the *Tonnerre* thundered and sent round shot screamed through the air. Something heavy and solid buried itself in the mizzenmast with a bone-shaking thump.

Sly dived behind a water barrel and put his hands over his ears.

Corrie felt weak.

I'm losing blood.

She unwound the stock from her neck, hoping the

long strip of cloth might serve to staunch the blood flowing from her chest. 'Handsomely now,' she said to the sail crew as the new canvas rose slowly up to the remounted topmast. 'Haul on those tacks!'

'That is the last new sail we have,' said Billy Brown quietly.

'I know,' said Corrie.

Billy frowned. 'You is hurt.'

'Yes,' said Corrie shortly. The world was breathing in and out like a huge pair of bellows. She stumbled back to the chaos of the quarterdeck and leaned on the binnacle.

It was time to say goodbye to the *Tonnerre*.

'You at the wheel, what's your name?'

'Green, sir.'

'Bring the ship about, Green. Steer for the gap between the island and the cliff.'

'Between the island and the cliff, sir,' said Green, and spun the wheel.

The wind caught the new canvas and the *Swift*'s bows swung away from the *Tonnerre*. As the *Swift* passed under the Frenchman's stern, Corrie heard her brother shout to the crews whose guns had been standing idle on the disengaged side. She heard a rumble as the fresh guns were run out, and then the air-shaking concussion as the guns discharged in a broadside that shattered the stern windows of the *Tonnerre* and blew the last of her splintered rudder clean off its gudgeons.

'Hooray for Captain Harriman!' shouted Billy Brown.

The seamen of the *Swift* paused in their work to doff their caps and cry 'Harriman! Harriman!' while stamping their feet on the deck to show their appreciation.

The fools think we are out of danger. I only wish it were true.

Somebody in the *Tonnerre* fired a musket.

The helmsman Green collapsed on the deck.

The wheel spun madly. The *Swift* fell away from the wind and headed back for the reef.

Corrie threw herself at the wheel, grabbed at the spokes and then spun them in the opposite direction to bring the *Swift* back on course. She hung on to the wheel for dear life. Sky and sea revolved around her.

My chest. The pain. I can hardly breathe.

'Jim!' she called out, desperately.

Her brother Jim ran to her side. 'You're hurt, Corrie,' he said, staring open-mouthed at her reddening shirt. He hadn't realized until this moment that his sister had been wounded, so busy had he been supervising the working of the guns.

'Don't worry about me,' she said. 'Green's been shot. Move him out of the way. Help me steer. We must pass inside the island.'

'Inside the island? Are you crazy? The tide's falling. There won't be enough water under our keel.'

'I know, but it's our best chance. By taking the inner passage, we shall have the island between us and the fort.'

'You're the captain,' said Jim, and he helped her spin the spokes to counter a breaking wave.

Spray hit them, blinding them both for a moment.

A crash of smashing timbers resounded around the bay.

For a moment Corrie thought she had run the *Swift* aground. But no, it was not her ship that was in trouble, not yet. It was the *Tonnerre*.

Corrie and Jim looked back in time to watch in horror as the *Tonnerre* struck the reef and rode up high on the barnacled rocks. They gazed spellbound as the French battleship tipped slowly and ponderously over onto her side. Hundreds of her sailors were thrown into the seething waves. Some were tossed upon the rocks while others swam for the shore. Some who could not swim thrashed about in the sea, and cried out for help.

Corrie and Jim looked at one another.

Corrie recalled how awful she had felt when the water had rushed into the bilge hole. 'I wish we could help them,' she said, and felt a desperate sadness.

We can't save them, but that does not make it any easier to sail away like this, listening to their despairing cries. Those poor sailors.

There could be no going back to assist the drowning, not this close to the fort. Corrie sighed. War was a grim business.

'The wheel, Jim,' said Corrie.

'Sorry,' said her brother, and dragged his eyes from the capsized French ship, and focused instead on what lay ahead: the narrow channel between the island and the shore, a channel boiling with angry, choppy waves.

XIX

ON THE far side of that churning narrow inner passage, Corrie glimpsed from time to time through the flying spindrift gay sparkles of aquamarine.

I must risk my ship to reach those faraway blue-green waters of the Bay of Plaisance. I hope we can reach them.

Without warning the seas off the starboard bow erupted in seven places, sending columns of white water and green weed towering into the air.

'The gunners in the fort have decided that we are not the *Havfruen*,' said Jim. He was close beside her, helping her with the wheel.

'Their forty pounders are trained to rake the main channel,' Corrie explained, as much to comfort herself as her brother. 'With any luck their gunners won't have time to adjust their elevation and to increase their powder charges by the amount they'll need to reach us this far away; and by the time they do have our range we should be well hidden by the island. That's my plan, at any rate, and the *Swift* seems to be handling well enough under the new storm topsail. I think we have a chance. I think we may get through to those blue waters of the bay if only we hold true. It wouldn't hurt to say a prayer.'

Jim answered her with a look of fresh resolve.

She saw him grip the spokes firmly with both hands and brace himself, his feet wide apart.

He was testing the ship.

Her brother had never steered the *Swift* before, nor had she, but they had steered the schooner *Maggie*

Rose in good weather and in bad.

'She is answering,' he shouted. 'We shall not need the relieving tackles, but I worry about all that water slopping about down there in the bilges.'

I know. Me, too. But what can we do?

There was no time to do anything about the bilges. They were already entering the dangerous passage behind the island, and the *Swift* was shouldering aside mountains of spuming water that threatened to lift up the whole ship and cast her bodily onto the rocks.

'There may be a blow back from the cliff,' she shouted, trying to stay on her feet. Her effort to staunch her wound had come to nothing. She was still bleeding. She clung to the wheel, and thought of her governess Mrs. Demeter, and of her stories of the Man of Many Tricks who had sacked Troy's sacred city, and of the grey-eyed goddess who kept her eye on him in times of peril.

Corrie felt the wind on her cheek. All that was left to propel the vessel forwards was the straining foretopsail. Here came the maelstrom. Waves began to charge at the *Swift* from all directions, making the steering very hard.

The sea has gone mad, and I'm bleeding to death.

Together Corrie and her brother fought to steer the ship. They felt the deck tremble under their feet as the *Swift* sagged down between two great water-worn turrets of stone. They heard the hull scrape past razor-sharp ledges studded with limpets.

Corrie looked up in awe at the foam-splattered cliffs of gneiss that towered to port and starboard. She felt the sting of the salt water on her lacerated chest. She helped her brother spin the spokes. The vessel heeled sharply. The lee rail vanished under a mass of slimy brown weed.

We are so close to the rocks. Odysseus had to choose between Scylla and Charybdis. He chose Scylla, and lost some of his sailors. I hope I shall not lose any of mine.

Lying over on her beam-ends, the *Swift* flew past a gaping sea cave where swallows had built their nests in crevices high in the stone walls. Inside the cave all was calm. A bright green pool of gently rippling water reflected bobbing light that decorated the smooth rock ceiling with ever-changing patterns of turquoise and gold.

How lovely! In the middle of these raging waters, we are given a glimpse of another world, still and passing strange. There is something alive in there. A monster. I can hardly believe what I am seeing.

In the shifting and shimmering light there sat a spotted behemoth that lifted its huge head and said 'Eeerp! Eeerp!' and then slid its gross body into the water and vanished.

A moment later the wheel bucked in their hands.

Determinedly, white-knuckled, they spun the spokes and sent the *Swift* hurtling by a streaming parapet. They caught a tantalizing glimpse of the blue-green of the open bay beyond.

'Nearly there!' shouted Jim.

Corrie nodded. Her chest hurt.

I don't want to lose my ship.

The *Swift* slewed her stern, dipped her bow, and met a great curling sea that rose up abruptly before them. The wall of water broke over the deck. They felt a sudden jarring beneath their feet as the keel of the *Swift* touched rock.

Corrie and Jim looked at one another. They had often run aground sailing their little dinghy in Quidi Vidi lake, but this was no dinghy they were sailing, and one more blow like that would surely break the *Swift*'s back.

'Starboard the helm!' ordered Corrie, and she and her brother leaned on the spokes and spun the wheel once more. 'Come on, you can do it,' she urged, speaking to the *Swift* directly for the first time.

Obediently, the *Swift* sprang aside, her strakes straining. Her topsail clapped like thunder in a back draught from the towering rock face. Like a shy horse that had refused her first jump, the *Swift* threw herself forward to leap once more, and this time she passed over the rock ridge without touching and burst free into the bright blue-green sea.

'Ease the helm,' said Corrie, taking her hands from the spokes and stepping away from the wheel. Jim could handle the steering by himself now. 'Keep her on this tack for as long as you can,' she said. 'We are out of range of the fort. The deck is yours. I must see to the wounded.'

'Better see to yourself first,' said Jim. 'You are covered in blood. I can't assist you with a wound like that, but you might try Anne Keeper.'

'Anne Keeper? She's just lost her husband. She's

shaking like a leaf.'

'Go to her. See what she can do. I saw her take that boy of hers to her cabin.'

'Maybe I'll drop by and ask how she's doing,' said Corrie and forced herself stand up straight and address her brother formally. 'Give Point Verde a wide berth, first lieutenant. The deck is yours.'

'Aye aye, captain,' said Jim. 'Steer wide of Point Verde.'

Corrie was pleased with her brother. She could rely on him to find someone to take the wheel now that the immediate danger had passed. He was her first lieutenant and there were a great many tasks to be done to put the ship to rights. The fight was over and the *Tonnerre* had been defeated, but Jim would have no rest, and nor would she.

Corrie could not *afford* to go on losing blood. She walked gingerly across the slanted deck, making every effort to ignore the stabbing pains in her chest.

She rapped on the door of the White Lady's cabin.

Anne Keeper's voice said 'Come in.'

Corrie opened the door, stepped over the sill, and then, holding onto the jamb so as not to fall, closed the door behind her carefully and leaned her back on it. She was exhausted.

'Oh, no,' said the White Lady, springing to her feet in a flurry of tulle, organdy and muslin. 'Not you, too. Take off that coat, Corrie, if you can? Here, sit down on my bunk. Let's have a look. Fraser, fetch my sewing kit.'

Corrie took off her hat and coat. She sat down

rather suddenly upon the broad bunk, and did her best to focus on Anne Keeper's boy Fraser.

She could see that the boy had been crying. She watched him pull himself together and open the family sea chest. He rummaged about until he found his mother's tear-shaped sewing case and pincushion. Her sewing case was open at the bottom, with a double leaf of red wool guarding a set of needles. The case was embroidered in silk and trimmed with gold cord and minute silk tassels. Fraser wiped his wet cheek with his sleeve and handed the handsome sewing kit to his mother.

'Fraser,' said Corrie, speaking firmly. 'I'm your new captain. I'm looking for a young man to train as an officer. Can you do what you're told?'

Fraser nodded.

'Speak up.'

'Yes, sir. Aye aye, sir,' said the boy, his eyes wide, staring at the blood welling from her chest.

'I have an important message for you to take to the ship's carpenter. Do you know the ship's carpenter?'

'Mr. Flight.'

'That's the man. Are you ready for the message?'

'Yes, sir,' said Fraser, and he looked at her expectantly.

'You're to tell Mr. Flight that he is to sound the well and to report to Captain Harriman on the quarterdeck. That's the message. Repeat it.'

'Captain's orders. Mr. Flight is to sound the well and report to Captain Harriman on the quarterdeck.'

'That's right. Off you go. Find Mr. Flight. Deliver

the message. I'm depending on you, Fraser. The whole ship is depending on you. Make sure my message reaches Mr. Flight.'

The boy's face lit up. 'Aye aye, sir,' he said and left the cabin in haste, banging the door behind him.

'That was well done,' said his mother. 'Fraser will feel better with something to do.' As she spoke Anne Keeper took a pair of sharp scissors from her kit and cut away the ragged remains of Corrie's shirt. 'It is a knife wound,' she said, examining the damage carefully. 'It looks to me like a shallow slash and not a deep puncture.'

'Can you take care of it for me?' asked Corrie. 'I have a ship to run.'

'The blow was struck under your right breast,' said Anne Keeper, 'but the knife was deflected from rib to rib. I shall begin by cleaning the wound. This is going to hurt. Bite down on this.' She handed Corrie a short length of thick leather trimmed from an old belt.

Corrie put the scrap of leather in her mouth and bit down hard. The leather tasted of the tannery where it had been cured.

Troude must have had a small blade hidden up his left sleeve. If ever I meet him again, I'll find a way to pay him back for this. If I live.

Many wounds festered for reasons unknown to medicine.

I trust this Grey-Eyed One, this White Lady Anne Keeper, who was widowed today.

Corrie studied Anne Keeper's steady long-fingered hands as they soaked a clean handkerchief in brandy, and went to work on the gaping gash. Anne had recovered from her shakes.

Pain!

She saw red. For something to think about, she wondered by what devious route Anne Keeper's bottle of brandy had been obtained. In all likelihood the strong drink had been brought over from France to England by the Cornish smugglers of St. Ives, and then purchased by some ship's chandler. After that the bottle must have been shipped to Newfoundland in one of the packet boats that supplied the station.

She wondered how much the Keepers had paid for the brandy, and why such potent spirits were used to clean a wound. It occurred to her that the very potency of the brandy might be efficacious. She knew that wine and spirits were safer to drink than water drawn from a well. Perhaps Anne Keeper was wise to dab a fresh wound with brandy, even if Corrie could not think of a reason why.

Corrie closed her eyes, trying not to think of what Anne Keeper's long, slender fingers were doing to her.

Ow! That stings! I must not cry out. I am the captain.

'I'll use my Coptic stitcher and some stout thread to draw the edges of the wound together,' said Anne Keeper, selecting a large curved needle from her housewife and wiping that needle with a swab soaked in brandy.

'You're going to stitch me up?' said Corrie, surprised.

Anne Keeper nodded. 'Yes, I am going to do a

little sewing. You'll feel the prick as the needle pierces your flesh. Try to relax. Keep still.'

Corrie did her best to relax, but her skin, tender and swollen, felt as if it were crying out in protest.

'There,' said Anne Keeper, tying off the thread and snipping away the ends with her scissors. 'You may expect the wound to go on bleeding for a while, but not as much as before. In an hour or two the bleeding should stop altogether. In the meantime, I shall wrap this long strip of cloth right around you to hold everything together. How do you feel?'

'Better. Thank you, Anne,' said Corrie. She watched Anne Keeper stopper the brandy, and return thread, scissors and needle to her sewing kit. Anne would have treated her husband's wounds in the same fashion had he survived the encounter with the *Tonnerre*. 'We are all going to miss Arthur,' Corrie said carefully. 'I don't have to tell you that he was a fine officer and a good man. He is a great loss to you and to Fraser, as well as to the ship. I'm sorry.'

'Fraser and I shall get over it,' said Anne Keeper. 'You had better change into this, captain,' she said, and passed a freshly laundered shirt to Corrie, a shirt that had belonged to her late husband, who would not need it again. 'We women are born free with equal rights to men, and have an equal right to fight.' Anne Keeper paused to look Corrie directly in the eye. 'Is that not so, captain?'

'Yes,' replied Corrie, pulling the shirt on over her head and wincing, 'and we are all in this fight together: you and me, Norah and Gladys, Billy Brown, the ship's cook, and that young girl Tomlinson who was shot when we cut out the *Galatée*. We are all in this together.' She reached for her coat and paused, wondering if this was a good moment to press Anne Keeper further.

'There are others?' she asked quietly.

Anne Keeper looked up and gave a barely perceptible nod.

'I'm glad,' said Corrie. She put her hat back on and reached for the door handle. 'We shall talk again soon, I trust.'

'I look forward to that, captain,' said Anne Keeper, and gave a wave of her hand.

Corrie left the cabin and closed the door. She stood for a moment, her fingers exploring her bandaged flesh. Her fingertips found the strange bumps of the White Lady's stitches. Extraordinary! She had been sewn up like a parcel.

Sobs came from the cabin. Anne Keeper was grieving.

I asked my question and she gave me her answer. There are other women in this ship who are disguised as men so that they may draw their pay. I shall keep a sharp eye out for those women, now that I'm their captain.

XX

THE wizened Mr. Flight, the ship's carpenter, was waiting on the quarterdeck with his report. 'Three feet of water in the well, sir,' he said, tugging his forelock in the fashion of the lower deck in the long gone days of Thomas Pellow and Zachary Peacock.

'Very well, sound the well again when the watch changes. I want to be sure we did no damage when we touched bottom.'

'Aye aye, captain,' said the carpenter.

Corrie regarded the old man carefully as he left the deck. She had noticed a twinkle in the carpenter's eye that seemed tell Corrie that she was the youngest captain Mr. Flight could recall in all of his long years of service. That boded well. She would be giving orders to many people older than herself in the hours and days ahead.

She turned to Jim, who had put Campbell at the wheel, and was now standing watch. 'Report,' she said.

'Billy and I have assigned parties to repair the damage to the rigging. The purser is supervising the treatment of the wounded. The sail maker's crew is stitching the bodies of the dead into bags. Some of them are French. We lost fourteen of our own people, including Redburn and Keeper. I've directed a party to begin clearing the decks. We're a mile off Point Verde and we need a course to steer. How's that wound of yours?'

'Mrs. Keeper has taken care of it, thank you. We need to find you a uniform,' she beckoned to young

Fraser. 'Fraser, you did a good job delivering that message. I'm appointing you midshipman as of this moment. Take command of this deck for a few minutes while Jim and I visit the captain's cabin. Can you do that?'

'Yes, sir,' said Fraser, displaying a child's sublime confidence in his own abilities.

'Good. You know where to find us if you need help,' she said.

Corrie and Jim found no marine on guard duty outside the captain's cabin. They pushed open the door and walked in.

'Everything looks just the same,' Corrie said, looking about her at the charts on the window seat, the books in the becket, the lantern swinging easily with the motion of the ship. 'It's as if the cabin were waiting for Redburn to come back.'

'He's not coming back,' said Jim. 'It's up to us now. Or rather, it's up to you. You're the captain. What do we do?'

'I'm not sure,' said Corrie, staring down at the chart with misgivings and running her eye over all of its spidery soundings and the warnings to mariners.

I must read Captain Redburn's instructions from their Lordships at the Admiralty. Where would he keep such instructions, I wonder?

'His clothes must be in his sleeping cabin,' said Jim, and strode boldly into that cabin to have a look.

Corrie's eye lit upon a locked drawer built into the table. She turned a small brass key in the lock and the drawer slid open as the ship heeled. She pulled out a packet weighted with shot and wrapped in canvas. She placed the packet on top of the chart, unwrapped the canvas and found a letter whose broken seal depicted the fouled anchor of the Admiralty.

I've found his instructions.

She carried the letter over to the upholstered bench under the great stern windows. Her wound forgotten in her excitement, she sat down on the bench to peruse the instructions given to Redburn, instructions that were now hers to obey in his stead.

'By Virtue of the Power and Authority to us given,' she read, 'we do hereby constitute and appoint you Captain of His Majesty's Ship the *Swift* willing and requiring you forthwith to go on board and take upon you the Charge and Command of Captain in her accordingly. Strictly Charging and Commanding all the Officers and Company belonging to the said ship subordinate to you to behave themselves jointly and severally in their respective Employments with all the Respect and Obedience unto you their said Captain.

'You are further requested and required to observe and execute as well the following Directions, that you shall without delay proceed to the isles of St. Pierre and of Miquelon, there to determine the presence or absence of the enemies of the Crown upon those shores, and to remove or destroy such enemies.

Whereafter, you are required to proceed to the Bay of Plaisance there to determine the presence of absence of the forces of Revolutionary France in that bay and to retake any Settlements or Fortifications those forces may have occupied there, and to capture or sink such enemy vessels as you may find there. Hereof nor you nor any of you may fail as you will answer the contrary at your peril. Given under our hands and the Seal of the Office of Admiralty this 14th day of July, in the Year of Our Lord 1800, by Command of their Lordships.'

For a few moments Corrie sat with the Admiralty letter in her hand, lost in thought. So that was their mission. There were those guns on the island of Saint Pierre to be silenced, and Fort Royal to be returned to English hands. She had no idea how she was to accomplish such extravagant aims optimistically penned by some pettifogging clerk in the Admiralty, but she thought she might begin by setting a course to take the *Swift* back to St. Pierre.

She stood up, returned the orders to the drawer, turned the brass key, and then bent over the chart. As best she could calculate, South West by South would be the course to give the helm with this wind blowing and with the tide on the ebb, but she would have to keep a sharp eye out tonight for surf breaking at the foot of Le Chapeau Rouge.

She looked up and saw a strange, well-dressed officer standing in the doorway leading to the sleeping cabin. For a moment she did not recognize him, but of course this was her brother, properly dressed at last as a naval officer. 'Jim! Is that really you?' she said delightedly, and clapped her hands. 'You handsome fellow!'

'Will I do? I'm afraid the hat doesn't fit me very well. I think Captain Redburn had a bigger head.'

'Who cares? You look like a proper first lieutenant, and I'm proud of you.' She paused. 'Lieutenant Harriman!'

Her brother came to attention. 'Yes, captain?'

'Go and relieve Midshipman Keeper before he runs us aground. Our course is South west by south. Look out for breakers at dawn. Stay well clear of the coast.'

'Aye aye, captain. South west by south, and keep out in the bay,' he said, and left the cabin.

As her brother closed the door behind him, Corrie thought back to the games he and she had played together at the bottom of the garden at home, acting out the parts of naval officers, calling out orders to imaginary seamen, fighting battles with imaginary enemies, and pelting one another with fallen apples.

I can feel Napoleon breathing down my neck. Bonaparte wants New France reborn, and I am here in the Gulf of Saint Lawrence to put a stop to his ambitions.

It dawned on Corrie as she sat there at the chart table that in all the ship, there was nowhere a body could find more peace and privacy than here in this very cabin that was now her own. Taxed by her wound, wearied by her new responsibilities, she rested her head on her arms.

She dreamed she was trapped in a cave with a giant. It was very dark in the cavern, and Corrie could hear the bleating of hungry ewes. Around the edges of the boulder that blocked the way out, the first light of dawn was faintly visible. She took up a bowl of strong, dark drink and walked carefully up to a one-eyed giant who had fallen asleep, his vast head cradled upon his arms. She came to the giant's face and kicked him as hard as she could on his nose.

'Wake up!' she shouted. 'Here's a surprise for you.'

'Who are you?' said the giant sleepily.

'Nobody,' said Corrie, and poured the strong drink down his vast throat.

She woke with a start. The captain's steward Harbottle had scurried into the cabin with a tray bearing a flagon of steaming Blue Mountain coffee and a boiled egg.

'Good morning, captain,' he said, placing the breakfast tray upon the chart table beside her. 'Light airs from the southeast. No sail in sight. The first lieutenant wants a word with you, sir, and the carpenter.'

'Thank you. I'll see them both, but first I must change out of this uniform.'

Harbottle tilted his head. 'His second-best coat might fit, and I have a shirt ironed, but I'm not sure about the breeches, sir.'

'Lay everything out on my bunk and I'll take care of myself.'

She could hardly let Harbottle dress her.

The coffee tasted good. Being a captain had its privileges. She peeled the egg and popped it in her mouth. Delicious.

She recalled the captain's instructions that she had read by the light of the lantern the night before.

Chewing on the egg, Corrie studied the chart, and

wished she knew the current position of the *Swift*.

I must have slept for hours. I must find out where we are. Perhaps Mr. Weevil knows.

She changed into the fresh uniform laid out by Harbottle and left the cabin. A Marine sentry who had been posted at her door snapped to attention as she passed. That was an improvement.

It was a dazzling morning. The glare of the sun bounced off the waves. A few charming puffy clouds, rimmed with golden light, decorated the horizon. There was a whiff of sea salt in the air. The Yeoman of the Sheets, Eaves, was at the wheel.

On the quarterdeck, Jim greeted her with a weary smile. Poor Jim. He had been up all night.

'Good morning, Mr. Harriman,' she said.

'Good morning, captain,' said Jim, and something about the look on his face told Corrie that her brother had not forgotten their childhood games together. There was a glint in his eye that reminded her of their many voyages. No doubt he was as amazed as she at the extraordinary good fortune that had led them to command a real warship in the middle of a real war.

She smiled back at him, mirroring his thoughts. Here they were, the pair of them, in charge of the *Swift*. Their childhood dream had come true, but grave responsibilities faced them on this beautiful morning.

'Report,' she said.

'The bodies have been prepared for burial and are laid out on the deck,' said Jim. 'Sly has been placed on report. Billy Brown has her people working on repairing the damage done to rigging. The sail maker's crew is patching the shot holes in the main course. The carpenter says there is only a foot of water in the hold now and it is not gaining.' He paused.

'And what?' said Corrie. She knew her brother well. She could see that there was something else he wanted to add.

'Mrs. Keeper is in her cabin,' said Jim. He lowered his voice. 'Weeping.'

Corrie took a deep breath. 'Let's get those burials over with.'

'All hands to witness burial!' shouted Jim, and his order was relayed throughout the ship.

Men, women and children crowded the deck. Anne Keeper stood beside her boy Fraser, now wearing the uniform of a midshipman. Gladys and Norah dabbed their eyes. Brown was solemn. Green was there, with one hand bandaged, with Campbell by his side. The Master-at-Arms, Jensen, had bared his head. Royal Marine Sergeant Deering came to attention, and barked an order to his men.

Hartnell the Purser had his muster book open and was recording the names of the deceased, adding the letters 'DD' standing for 'Discharged, Dead' after every one of fourteen names.

Steward Harbottle and the Cook were weeping. Both had been fond of Captain Redburn. John Eaves, the Yeoman of the Sheets, kept his eye on the compass card and his hands on the wheel. Even in solemn moments like these the ship had to be steered and the lookouts had to stay sharp.

The Master was among the crowd, looking more

bewildered and puzzled than he had yesterday, the poor old soul. Corrie read the words of the service from the late captain's prayer book, and finished by saying 'We therefore commit their bodies to the deep.'

Jim gave a discreet signal and the men he had assigned to the solemn duty of burying the dead went to work, and the bodies of the fourteen who had lost their lives in the fight with the French slid down the boat ramp. Each corpse had been sewn up in an individual hammock and weighted with shot. The bodies splashed into the sea, and vanished into the depths.

I must not look sad. A captain must be unmoved at all times.

After the service, Corrie gave Anne Keeper a big hug and shook hands with Anne's son. 'Your father was a good man, Fraser,' she said, 'and I hope you will be as brave and resourceful an officer.'

The crowd dispersed. Some went below, some into the rigging. Others remained on deck to continue repairing the many ravages done to the ship during the action.

Corrie walked to the quarterdeck. Her sore chest felt stiff but hurt less than yesterday.

Soon Mikkel Jensen, the Master-at-Arms, brought before Corrie the miserable figure of Augustus Sly, in ankle and wrist irons.

'Warrant Officer Sly, sir,' said Jensen, coming to attention. 'For cowardice in the face of the enemy.'

'Speak up, Sly,' said Corrie. 'Why did you hide in that roll of sail?'

'I was going to wait until them Frenchies boarded

us,' said Sly, 'and then jump out of hiding and surprise them. You've no right to chain me up like this.'

'You address me as "captain." How were you planning to attack the French, Sly? You had no weapon with you.'

Sly rattled his chains 'You can't do this to me,' he said. 'You're not even a real captain. You're just a girl.'

'Did you or did you not have a weapon with you when you hid in the roll of storm canvas?'

'Maybe I did,' said Sly, with a crafty look in his eyes, 'and then again maybe I didn't.'

'Maybe I didn't, *captain*.'

'Maybe I didn't, *captain*,' said Sly cheekily.

'I can hang you right now, Sly,' said Corrie. 'You have contravened the Articles of War by hiding yourself away.'

'You can't do nothing to me, missie,' said Sly. 'I'm a warranted officer.'

Corrie clenched her fists.

Shall I hang this rude and cruel man? He tried to have Jim and I hanged on our very first day in the ship. I should love to order a noose be put round his neck. But what he says is true. He does have a warrant.

'Mr. Jensen,' said Corrie. 'Sly is to be taken to the orlop. He is to be chained to the bilge engine, and his duty henceforth and for the remainder of this voyage, shall be to pump the bilges dry. For as long as he performs this duty, you are to give him food and water.'

'Aye aye, sir,' said Jensen, and led Sly away.

'You can't do this to me,' shouted Sly, his fat

cheeks red with rage. 'I got friends in high places, I have. I should be the bloody captain, not you. A woman's no good for running a ship. You'll be sorry you didn't hang me, missie. You wait and see.'

'Master-at-Arms,' said Corrie, ignoring Sly. 'You did an excellent job of impersonating Swarbrek. I shall mention your name in my report to the Admiral.'

'Thank you, sir,' said Jensen.

'How good are you with a sextant, Jensen?'

'Not bad, I think, my captain.'

'Would you help me take my noon sights?' said Corrie.

'Yes, sir,' said the Dane, a smile spreading across his face. 'I teach you good.'

'Carry on then. Take this wretched man below before I change my mind and hang him.'

'Ja, captain,' said Jensen, and dragged Sly away.

'See no harm comes to him,' she said quietly to Jim. 'I don't want him tormented.'

'I'll see that he is treated better than he treated us,' said Jim, and then he glanced thoughtfully at the horizon. 'When the French authorities hear that we sunk the *Tonnerre*, what will they do?'

'They will send a squadron to destroy us,' said Corrie. 'Jim, you have been up all night. Go and put your head down. You may use the Second Lieutenant's cabin.'

'We joined the navy,' said her brother, 'and we sank an enemy ship.' He yawned.

'Go and turn in, Jim,' said Corrie. 'I mean it. I'll keep an eye on things.'

Jim went below.

Corrie stood on the quarterdeck with her hands clasped behind her back, wondering where their parents were and what they would think if they learned that she was now in command of a ship. In time of war, extraordinary burdens are sometimes placed on young shoulders.

As a child she had been enchanted by the notion of entering the secret world of the Royal Navy, a world forbidden to women, and of daring the boys to do their worst. She had dreamed of riding stormy seas and of fighting fierce enemies. Now that dream had become reality.

She commanded one of His Majesty's ships, and was responsible for the lives of scores of men, women and children. In a few moments, she would begin the real work of a captain. She would go down into the depths of the ship and make sure that they were treating Sly properly. She would find out why the new hands were still quartered in the stable, when they ought to have been issued hammocks days ago. Some of the wounded were in critical condition, she had heard. She would visit them and hold their hands.

She stood up straight, battling the pain in her chest.

Close hauled on the starboard tack, the *Swift* buried her bowsprit in a wave and sent a curtain of spray flying into the air.

Corrie was thankful for that spray.

With so much water flying about, nobody will notice that I am crying.

COMING SOON

Experience Napoleon's wrath and feel the deck heave beneath your feet as Frigate Captain Jean-Pierre Troude and his Red Lady descend in fury upon Jim and Corrie Harriman to avenge themselves on our heroes in the breath-taking sequel to 'Midshipman Harriman'

LIEUTENANT HARRIMAN

by Anthony Barton

BY THE SAME AUTHOR

THE BAT RIDER ADVENTURES

Matthew John's adventures may be downloaded in English or Spanish to your mobile device, phone, tablet or e-book reader from Apple, Barnes & Noble, Sony, Kobo, Diesel, Scrollmotion and Smashwords.com

The Bat Rider tales in chronological order are:

BAT RIDER AND THE CAVE OF OOMBA
BAT RIDER AND THE BACK OF BEYOND
BAT RIDER AND THE LOONY MOON
BAT RIDER AND THE DEN OF BAAGH
BAT RIDER AND THE PIT OF MORMOOPS
BAT RIDER AND THE LAIR OF HYOU
BAT RIDER AND THE BIG BAD BAT
BAT RIDER AND THE TIME OUT OF MIND
BAT RIDER AND THE CITY OF GHOSTS
BAT RIDER AND THE GECKO BOGO
BAT RIDER AND THE LORD OF THE LOCUSTS
BAT RIDER AND THE FOREST FIRE

Three Bat Rider omnibus volumes are available from Amazon.com in print and as Kindle e-books:

BAT RIDER
THE YUMI TREES
THE BAT RIDERS OF YUMI

BAT RIDER AND THE CAVE OF OOMBA
is also available as a free audio serial in 8 episodes with music and bat squeaks by Siri Arnet from Podiobooks.com

*A Book for Boys and Girls
by the Same Author*

HORSY-HOPS
by Anthony Barton

Horsy-hops is a delightful story for children in pictures and verse. A little girl meets the Horsy-hops monster and his friends. Instead of being afraid, she makes friends with them and asks them to her birthday party.

'Children will relish the book's arrant silliness while parents savor the new phrases.'

-- Quill and Quire

'Added bonuses are instructions for playing turtles and the score and lyrics for the Horsy-hops Song. Enjoy.'

-- The Globe and Mail

Horsy-hops is available in print from

Breakwaterbooks.com

Made in the USA
Charleston, SC
05 February 2013